Olof and Lena Landström

WILL GOES TO
THE POST OFFICE

Translated by Elisabeth Dyssegaard

R&S
BOOKS

Stockholm   New York   London   Adelaide   Toronto

JELAN

Rabén & Sjögren Stockholm
Translation copyright © 1994 by Rabén & Sjögren
All rights reserved
Originally published in Sweden by Rabén & Sjögren
under the title *Nisse går till posten,* text and illustrations copyright © 1993
by Olof and Lena Landström
Library of Congress catalog card number: 94-66898
Printed in Denmark
First edition, 1994

ISBN 91 29 62950 0

A. Title

Will is going to the post office to pick up a package.
It is from Uncle Ben.

Karen and Peter are sitting on the steps,
playing ticktacktoe.

Will shows them the card from the post office.

Karen and Peter come along.

It's not far, just a few blocks.

"There it is," says Peter.

"How lucky that the line is short," says Will.

The post office is cool
and crammed full of packages.
"I hope it's something big," says Peter.

Now it's Will's turn.

Will wonders which package is his.

Perhaps it **is so** small that it has gotten lost.

"Wow!" says Karen.

How lucky that the package isn't heavy!

But it is difficult to walk when you can't see.

Here comes John. He wants to help, too.

And here is Susan. She is on her way to buy milk.
"I'll hold the door!" she says.

Five more steps!

"My goodness!" says Mama.

There are a lot of knots.
Mama thinks it's best to use scissors.

Is there nothing but paper in the box?

No, there's something else.

It's a globe! A globe with a light!

But it's best if it's dark when you turn it on.
So it can shine properly.

"We have to write to Uncle Ben
and say thank you," says Mama.

THE DESIGN CONCEPT SERIES

Elements of Design
TEXTURE George F. Horn
COLOR AND VALUE Joseph A. Gatto
SPACE Gerald F. Brommer
SHAPE AND FORM Albert W. Porter
LINE Jack Selleck

Principles of Design
BALANCE AND UNITY George F. Horn
CONTRAST Jack Selleck
EMPHASIS Joseph A. Gatto
MOVEMENT AND RHYTHM Gerald F. Brommer
PATTERN Albert W. Porter

Emphasis

Joseph A. Gatto
Art Teacher, Los Angeles, California

DAVIS PUBLICATIONS, INC.
Worcester, Massachusetts U.S.A.

To my father, 'Lo' and Michael

Printed in the United States of America
Library of Congress Catalog Card Number: 75-21112
ISBN: 0-87192-075-1

Printing: Worzalla Publishing Company Inc.
Binding: Worzalla Publishing Company Inc.
Type: Optima Medium
Graphic Design: Penny Darras, Thumbnail Associates

Consulting Editors: Gerald F. Brommer, George F. Horn,
Sarita R. Rainey

10   9   8   7   6   5   4

All photographs by the author unless otherwise noted.

Contents

6

Introduction

What do you consider significant? Why? Did you feel that way last year? Emphasis is an expression and extension of your mind and emotions. Emphasis is also the art principle by which the visual components are tied together through dominance and subordination. Through emphasis, the artist attempts to control the sequence in which visual events are observed or the amount of attention which is paid to them.

You are confronted with many ideas, situations and moods, some of which are more important than others. To these you assign a different set of values and, thus, you react to them more keenly.

In some cases, the ideas you considered important a short time ago have already lost some of their significance. Situations that seemed insurmountable at one time are now, perhaps, only distant memories. They have lost their emphasis.

We do know that emphasis changes with time, geographic location, socio-economic conditions, philosophy and with countless other factors. Only you can determine what is important or what is to be emphasized and how much you will allow it to change your life, for emphasis is a *point of view*.

Of course, sometimes you are told what is important and to what you should give preeminent value. By and large, however, emphasis is dependent on you, the individual. Unfortunate are those societies where stress is placed on a single philosophy.

Sometimes you give prominence to situations intuitively and spontaneously, much the same as some artists do; other times you react in a deliberate, more reflective manner. Regardless of which direction you take, you do emphasize things either for brief periods of time or for a longer duration, depending on accompanying circumstances.

Just as you emphasize certain things in your life that are more important to you, the artist also emphasizes certain parts of his work because they are more important. This book will attempt to show how you can become aware of these centers of interest and points of emphasis around you, and how to use this information in your art work.

Achievements in space, political and economic considerations, all undergo a shift in priorities. Emphasis of ideas and preferences change with time. Photograph courtesy of the National Aeronautics and Space Administration.

The forces of nature provide us with the opportunity for a personal encounter. Importance placed on understanding these forces, physical conditioning and a desire for achievement offer rewarding experiences. Photograph courtesy of Helmut Wielander.

Emphasis: A Point of View

Today, young people are giving emphasis to a wide range of philosophies, in addition to those traditionally held.

In the process of reclaiming our cities, future planners must consider the preservation of livable green space. Thus, the emphasis will be on building up instead of out. Photograph courtesy of United California Bank.

The world's food supply seemed inexhaustible at one time. However, population growth, weather conditions, abuse of natural resources, blight and pests have changed the situation. Importance must now be placed on new food supplies, greater land yield and the cultivation of the oceans' resources. Furthermore, emphasis must be placed on consolidating efforts to solve mutual concerns.

The wise use of leisure time is as important as work or school. In prosperous cultures, where working hours are becoming shorter, increased emphasis has been placed on ways to use this time, including the exploration of different art media.

The piece of cloth hanging from the barbed wire accentuates its presence, thus preventing possible injury from the otherwise unseen wire. Emphasis is on concern for others.

The potential for learning is different for each individual. Some learning experiences are visual while other experiences emphasize audio responses.

Emphasis on the selection of toys for young children contributes to their understanding of work and play and to the development of useful habits necessary for growth.

The drawings of young children often reveal the important aspects of their experiences. Many insights can be gained by observing the forms they emphasize. The same can be said for your art work and the work of prominent artists.

The sculptor, Henry Moore, gave preeminent value to the human form. His sculpture is the result of a lifetime spent seeking an understanding of an art form of importance to him.

You may remember Alexander Calder as the American artist who invented the mobile and, thus, gave emphasis to sculpture that moved. This airplane, decorated with his painting, gives importance to the philosophy of service rendered by the airline. Photograph courtesy Braniff International Airlines, Dallas, Texas.

The emphasis placed on the inventive use of our resources has resulted in a high standard of living for many people. Photograph courtesy of Bethlehem Steel Corporation.

Emphasis on beautiful, functional design gives prestige to the designer and the manufacturer, as well as to the owner of this car. Photograph courtesy of British Leyland Motors Inc.

The preservation of our natural resources and concern for a healthy environment are gaining import with an increasing number of people. Tantamount to preserving the environment is that it be beneficial and functional for our use. Photograph courtesy of Del Monte Properties, Pebble Beach, California.

An artist, like any other member of society, is influenced by the same forces, tensions and anxieties. Kathe Kollwitz placed importance on how she felt about what she saw. She emphasized personal expression in her art. *No More War,* Kathe Kollwitz. Photograph courtesy Galerie St. Etienne, New York.

Graffiti artists give emphasis to their philosophy, their sense of belonging and their individuality.

PLACEMENT

We read from left to right. Placement of the group of flowers to the right in the photograph gives the composition emphasis. We must look more carefully for the subordinate forms of the bee and flower buds.

The placement of the bolt and washer on the picture plane creates variation in the division of space. The round form is given additional emphasis by value contrast and by the rectangular forms of the wood.

The round form of the pocket watch dictates that emphasis be given to harmonious enrichment. The scroll work is congruous with the watch and the forms on the back.

SURFACE ENRICHMENT

CONTRAST OF VISUAL ELEMENTS

The recessed round form, the bolt and the diagonal cast shadow are all in opposition to the vertical texture lines. Contrast gives interest through variation.

The broken glass, charred wood and variation of color are in direct contrast with the smooth surface and edge line of the real estate sign. Emphasis is on contrasting visual elements.

The painting of *The Old King* by Georges Rouault reflects his early training as a stained-glass window-maker. Contrasting color and pigment texture are emphasized. Courtesy Museum of Art, Carnegie Mellon University, Pittsburgh.

Some of the old blocks are worn from play and exposure to the natural elements, resulting in reduced contrast. Contrasting the visual elements is necessary for emphasis.

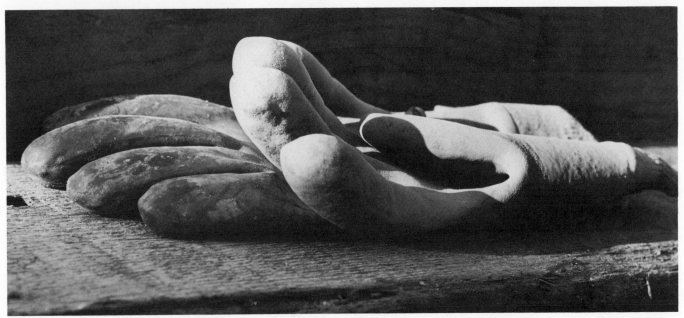

The workman's gloves are surrounded by background areas that are not strong visually. Subordinating the background gives emphasis to foreground forms.

Another way to give emphasis is to isolate forms in space on the pictorial surface. Isolation also creates the illusion of depth.

SUBJECT ISOLATION

22

Emphasis is gained by having the background less conspicuous than an object shown against it. An object is more easily seen against a simple background as in the drawing by Kathe Kollwitz. *Home Worker,* Kathe Kollwitz. Charcoal drawing, 22½'' x 16''. Courtesy of Los Angeles County Museum of Art, Graphic Arts Council Fund.

The toy bear appears to be separated from the nearby forms that are blurred or lack contrast. Emphasis is achieved by allowing ample space around forms.

SPACE AROUND FORMS

DISTORTION AND THE UNUSUAL

The artist, Amadeo Modigliani, was influenced by African Art. He gave emphasis to forms in painting by distortion. *Portrait of a Young Woman,* Amadeo Modigliani. Oil on canvas, 18″ x 11″. Yale University Art Gallery, bequest of Mrs. Kate Lancaster Brewster.

The distortion of the visual elements deserves study and attention. We give importance to forms that are unusual or out of context.

The pigeon stretching its wing and leg attracts attention because it is different and, thus, gives emphasis to that area of the pictorial surface.

Surrealist painters go beyond the real, often painting the unusual or unexpected in addition to the dream. *The Persistence of Memory* (Persistance de la memoire) 1931, Salvador Dali. Oil on canvas, 9½" x 13". Collection, The Museum of Modern Art, New York. Given anonymously.

COMPARISON OF SIZES AND NUMBERS

Easily recognized forms facilitate visual judgments. One look at the server's hands indicates the size of the glasses of ice cream.

Emphasis is achieved by the appearance of many similar forms.

The dimensions of the pipes and crane are underscored when compared with the men standing on them. Photograph courtesy of The Owl Companies.

When many forms appear on the pictorial surface, emphasis is achieved by reinforced concepts.

REPETITION AND PROPORTION

Proportion is comparing the size relationship of one form to another. Emphasis is large against small.

Important safety factors are reinforced by repetition.

The forms of the plow blades achieve emphasis through repetition. Additional interest is achieved by the varied reflections in the polished surfaces.

The painter, Diego Rivera, stressed repetition and simplification in his paintings as they were intended for the poor and illiterate. Emphasis by repetition and simplification heightens the emotions. *Flower Day* 1925 *Dia de Flores*, Diego Rivera. Oil on canvas, 47½'' x 58''. Los Angeles County Museum of Art, Los Angeles County Funds.

The blur created by the spokes of the tire is emphasized by the absence of significant movement of the bicycle fork.

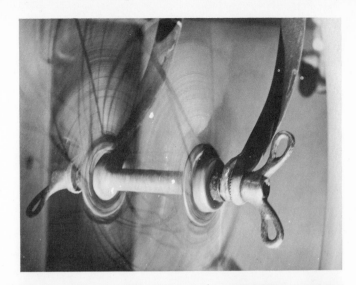

The concentration of short, quick, diagonal brush strokes accentuates the movement of forms in the painting. Through this expression of dynamic energy and movement, the Futurists led the way to early cinema. *The City Rises* (1910), Umberto Boccioni. Oil on canvas, 6' 6½'' x 9' 10½''. Collection, The Museum of Modern Art, New York, Mrs. Simon Guggenheim Fund.

The time exposure emphasizes the many directions and movements made by neon, auto and street lights.

DIRECTION AND MOVEMENT

CONVERGING LINES

The dark value of the bridge tower restrains the eye, forcing it to the converging lines of the street and to a possible point of emphasis.

The vertical line of the telephone pole, the wires and service ropes create converging lines, leading the eye to the serviceman.

Convergence of lines in the plant achieves emphasis on the picture plane and imparts dominance to that point. The eye finds it difficult to resist the point from which lines radiate.

In the poster, the many diagonal lines meet and converge at the head of the figure, giving emphasis to the emotional scream. Collection of the author.

CREATING A CENTER OF INTEREST

The twisted wire, the space activated by it and the old shipping label create a dominant image and assume the center of interest. In your art work, a center of interest should be emphasized.

The center of interest on a pictorial surface is composed of subordinate visual elements.

Functions of Emphasis

When our normal frame of reference is interrupted, a major point of view is established. The painting by Hiram Williams employs an aerial view to give emphasis to the walking figure. *Incubus,* Hiram Williams. Courtesy National Collection of Fine Arts, Smithsonian Institution.

Symbolism, familiarity, location and lack of visual activity on the brick wall, all contribute to the flag's assuming the center of interest.

The clotheslines create movement to the right, emphasizing that side of the composition. The immediate area would be sufficient for subject matter placement. The clothespins add subordinate movement, forming other interest areas on the pictorial surface.

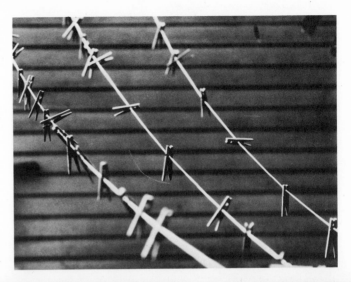

Optical movement can be produced in a painting. Body position of the figures, eye contact and value contrast, all draw attention to the dog. *After the Hunt,* Winslow Homer. Watercolor on paper, 24¾″ x 18¾″. Courtesy Los Angeles County Museum of Art, Paul Rodman Mabury Collection.

The cast shadow of the pipe establishes a diagonal movement, carrying the eye through the composition.

The figure across the street creates optical movement on the pictorial surface and the illusion of space. Illusion of space is created by emphasis on size variation and higher placement on the picture plane.

CREATING OPTICAL MOVEMENT

The visual elements surrounding the outline of the window are subordinated because the construction of the window suggests space and the variation is contained in a small area.

Some Oriental artists established nature as the dominant theme in their paintings while de-emphasizing human form.

The artist, Georges Braque, subordinated form in this painting by emphasizing small bright areas of pigment. *Boats on the Beach,* Georges Braque. Oil on canvas, 27½" x 19½". Courtesy Los Angeles County Museum of Art, Gift of Anatole Litvak.

The strong side lighting from the sun actually de-emphasizes the design of the fence. As the sun moves, the emphasis changes, establishing different visual dominance and subordinance.

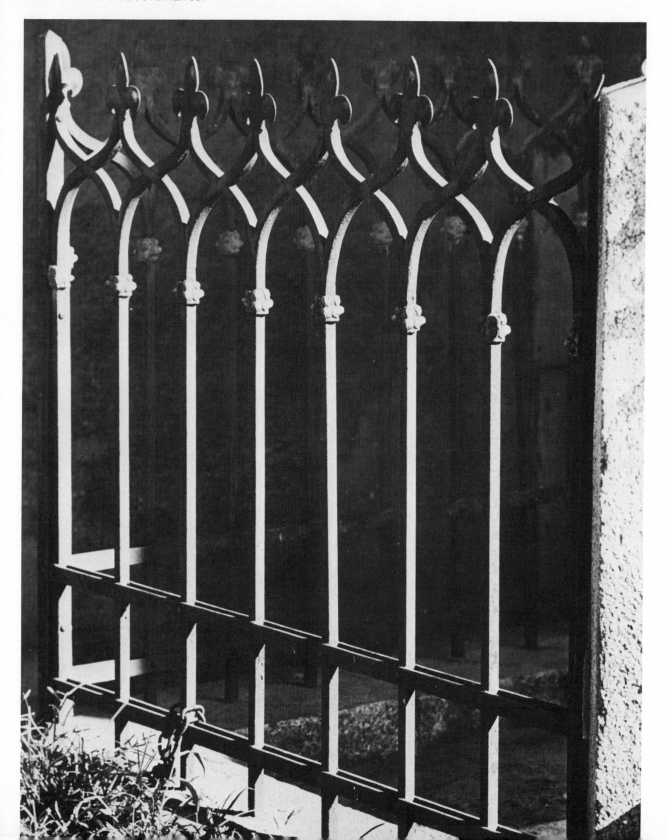

Similar lines, forms and textures are contrasted with the dominant light and dark values. Together, they complement each other and create unity.

The similar distortion of forms in the window glass, contrasted with the straight window frame, unifies the visual elements by establishing dominant and subordinate elements.

UNIFICATION OF VISUAL ELEMENTS

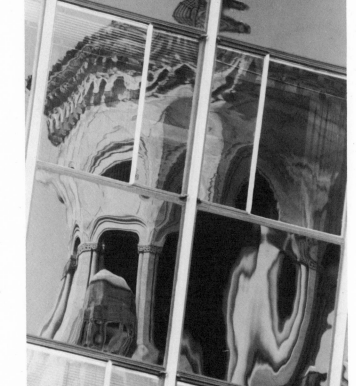

The curved line of the ladder on the oil-storage tank seems to move from the background to the foreground, unifying space.

The division of space, variation of value and texture have sufficient contrast and variation to create unification of the visual elements. Emphasis is achieved by contrasting art elements. *Vue De Marseilles*, Nicholas de Stael. Oil on canvas, 35" x 51". Courtesy Los Angeles County Museum of Art, Gift of the Estate of Hans de Schulthess.

Photographic techniques developed to extend the range of human vision demonstrate the beauty and interaction of the visual elements of the flowers. Photograph courtesy of Eastman Kodak Company.

The balance of the visual elements and similar surface treatment link together the art elements found on the old car.

The peeling paint provides sufficient change among the door, the window glass and the window frames. Contrast and placement give emphasis to the door, while subordinating and linking the other visual elements.

LINKING VISUAL ELEMENTS

Similar forms, colors, textures and display techniques demonstrate how a lack of understanding of the visual elements creates lack of emphasis.

LACK OF EMPHASIS

Confusion results when the visual elements are equally emphasized. Many of the signs have lost their identity and fail to achieve their potential function.

Beautiful forms do not make the pictorial surface aesthetic. Overemphasis on similar forms, colors, textures and lack of contrast creates a monotonous composition.

CONFUSION AND CHAOS

Both the flower and the peeling paint of the wall are similar in surface appearance. The forms blend together and camouflage each other, whereas contrast of the visual elements would have created emphasis.

The irregular growth and reduced contrast between the flower and the background shrubs contribute to visual confusion. No one art element truly dominates the pictorial surface. The artist must learn which elements to isolate and emphasize.

The apparent chaos in the junk pile is an example of too many similar forms, colors and textures. Lack of variation and contrast establishes visual disorder.

The structure of the billboard is visually active and detracts from the function of the display. Overemphasis on a single art element creates visual disharmony.

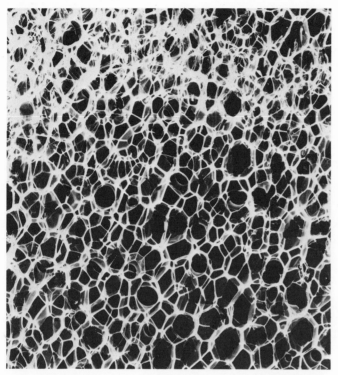

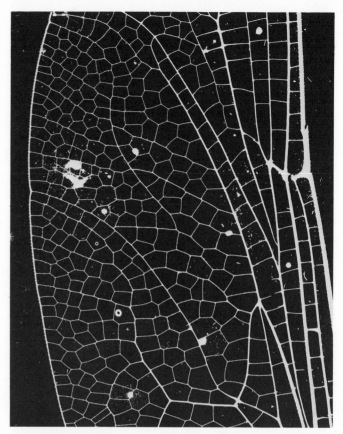

A thin slice of styrofoam was projected on photography paper, allowing us to study the structure of this material.

The variation of lines and negative shapes is emphasized when the dragonfly wing is projected.

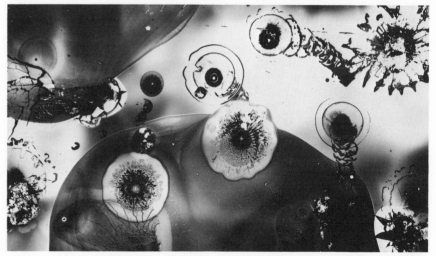

Soot from a hobby lamp using motor oil is allowed to cover a small piece of glass and is enriched with various materials. Concepts about abstract design are emphasized.

What to emphasize, how much to emphasize and where to place emphasis is up to you, the individual. Increased knowledge about the art elements and principles will help you make the decisions.

There are many ways to gain an understanding of design and to make exciting discoveries of the environment. For example, obtain some small cardboard mounts similar to transparency mounts. Select forms from nature, forms made by man and experiment with original arrangements and interpretations. Mount these forms between clear acetate or plastic wrap and staple them between the cardboard mounts. Then project the transparencies with a slide projector or make them into photographic prints.

Emphasis and the Elements of Design

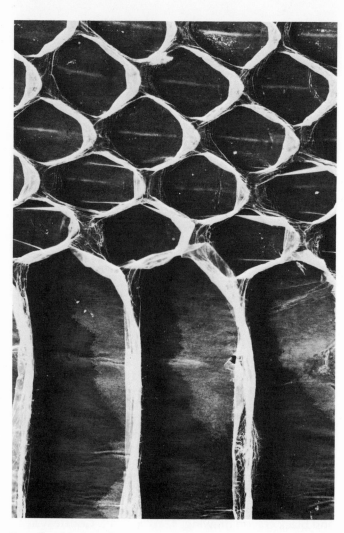

India ink, manipulated on the surface of the acetate, reveals interesting forms. Emphasis is placed on the discovery and invention of forms.

Reptile skin has dominant and subordinate elements of design.

The potential for discovering new forms in the environment is infinite. A case in point is offered by the flexible tubing and compressed metals in a junkyard. Emphasis is placed on surface tensions and on the interaction of one form with another. Courtesy of Jason Hailey. Selective Eye® II, Number 4.

Sophisticated variation of the visual elements, with emphasis on the bird and tree forms, helps create additional surface enrichment, as well as interesting optical movement. Tapestry, collection of the author.

Photographic techniques permit us to extend our perception of nature. With awareness on our part, we can determine the function of forms. Photograph courtesy of Eastman Kodak.

The bright red-orange of the flower form achieves dominance by the advancement of the warm color in opposition to the recessive cool, background color.

VALUE

The sun's position is in a constant state of flux. The different angles create new forms as seen on the bridge porthole. We give emphasis to the variations in nature and employ them in our art work.

The beauty of the nautilus shell demonstrates the significance of functional forms contributing to the total form of the shell. The subtle variation of the forms create additional elegance. Photograph courtesy of Eastman Kodak.

The sun's angle on the water, hose and stone demonstrates the wide range of values possible. Emphasis is on the variation between light and dark.

The eye is quickly attracted by strong contrasts of light and dark or by contrasting color. One way to achieve emphasis is to call attention to an object by contrast.

The artist, Franz Kline, emphasizes the separation between dark and light to describe less of what is objectively seen and more of what is subjectively felt. The contrast of value is indicative of the forces and tensions of the 20th Century. *The Ballantine,* Franz Josef Kline. Oil on canvas, 72″ x 72″. Los Angeles County Museum of Art, estate of David E. Bright.

The leaf forms contrast in color with the blue sky. The contrasting warm and cool colors give movement to the picture plane while emphasizing space.

The strong backlighting of the sun on the leaf creates a center of interest. Emphasis is on warm and cool color contrast.

COLOR

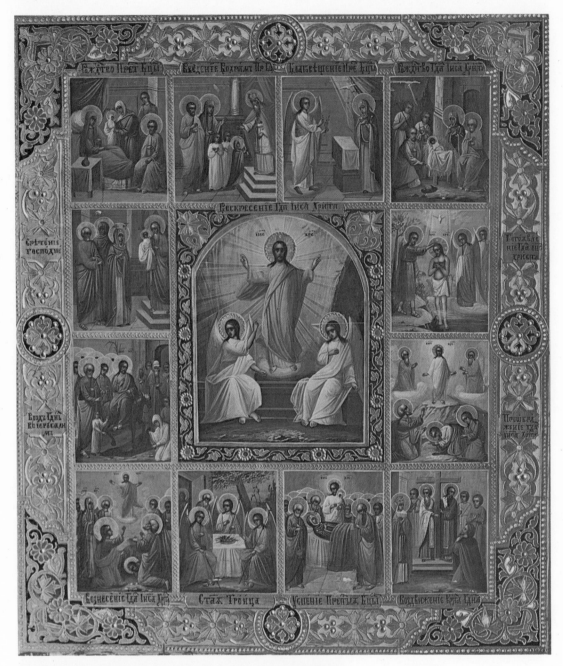

The icon painting demonstrates the emphasis achieved
by warm and cool contrast of color, with each panel
using recessive blue pigment contrasted by advancing
warm reds, oranges and yellows. Russian Icon, Artist
unknown. Collection of author.

There are many ways of creating the illusion of space on the pictorial surface. One way is to emphasize over-lapped forms, as with the lamp over the window.

SPACE

Shallow space or flatness is created when emphasis is placed on lines that are parallel to the edges of the pictorial surface.

The same subject matter photographed at angles to the edges of the picture plane creates the illusion of space. The greater angles suggest deeper space.

Unusual views, like low angle or extreme high angle, give emphasis to spatial concepts because the normal frame of reference is interrupted. Photograph courtesy of Union Camp Corp., Savannah, Georgia.

The artist, Camille Pissarro, used contrasting sizes, straight against curved, and placed many forms on the upper portion of the picture plane to create the illusion of space. Emphasis is achieved by contrasting visual elements. *Place Du Theatre Francais,* Camille Pissarro. Oil on canvas, 36½" x 28½". Los Angeles County Museum of Art, Mr. and Mrs. George Gard DeSylva Collection.

The beauty of paint and paper peeling from fences and wall surfaces is realized through the medium of photography. The artistic achievement is sometimes intellectually realized and often intuitively felt. Courtesy Jason Hailey, Selective Eye® I, Number 21, *Paint on Metal Surface*, Los Angeles 1958. Museum of Modern Art, New York, Permanent Collection. Also collection of author.

By observing the inventive manipulation of the art elements, you may gain an understanding of what the artist emphasized. The exploration of surface phenomena by the photographer, Jason Hailey, evolved from an interest in hieroglyphics and in abstract expressionist painting. Courtesy Jason Hailey, Selective Eye® I, Number 14.

TEXTURE AND DOTS

The optical mixture of colored dots was emphasized by the Pointillist painters. In realizing this process, the Pointillist painters seemed to anticipate the four-color, halftone process by which almost all full-color photographs are reproduced in mass printing. *Sunday Afternoon On The Island Of La Grande Jatte,* Georges Seurat. Oil on canvas, 81" x 120⅜". Courtesy The Art Institute of Chicago.

The dot is a vehicle for visual communication; and when many dots appear on a surface, optical fusion results. Communication is then possible. The two photographs demonstrate the potential of dots to create imagery.

Emphasis: How It Is Used

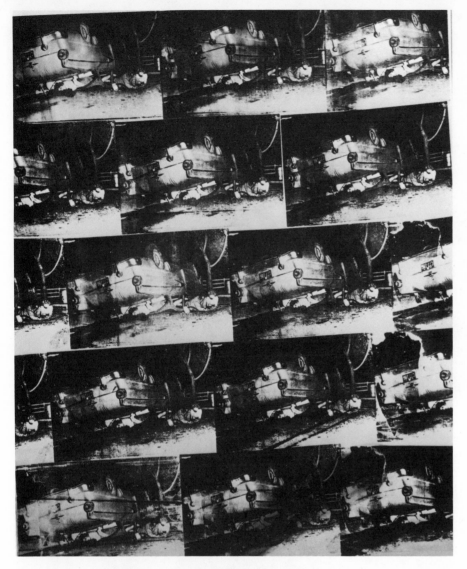

The artist, Andy Warhol, uses repetition to achieve emphasis, overcoming indifference or resistance and demonstrating how our technical advances have dominated moral and aesthetic considerations. *5 Deaths 17 Times,* Andy Warhol. Silkscreen on canvas, 104" x 82". Courtesy Leo Castelli Gallery, Private Collection.

PHOTOGRAPHY

The photographer, Ansel Adams, emphasizes the idealization of nature and concern for the preservation of natural resources with perfectly rendered photographs that combine artistic sensibility with scientific understanding and know how. *Point Sur Monterey Coast California,* Ansel Adams. Courtesy Ansel Adams and Polaroid Corp., from permanent collection of Polaroid Corp.

MASON PROFFIT
COME & GONE

Package design increases in importance as more products are exposed to an ever competitive market. The record jacket symbolizes the moods, ideas and emotions of times come and gone. It is possible to emphasize ideas, as well as the art elements. Courtesy Warner Bros. Records Inc. Photography Albert McKenzie Watson.

The logo is used by large firms to emphasize product identity and services. In this office building, it serves to locate where information can be obtained. Courtesy Albert C. Martin and Associates. Photography Wayne Thom.

The unusual and unexpected are paramount in this advertisement for an airline. Mood and emotion are photographically emphasized. Courtesy Cunningham & Walsh Inc., San Francisco. Photography Hans Hoefer.

The poster for a film festival is an example of direct visual communication. Emphasis is on design that is simple enough to be easily and quickly perceived. The selection of colors heightens the festive event, while the treatment of the writing is done with conviction, as one would note an important event on a calendar. Courtesy Saul Bass & Associates, Inc., Los Angeles, California.

GRAPHIC DESIGN

INDUSTRIAL DESIGN

The necessity and function of a form often determine what is emphasized. The large construction crane seen in a gasoline storage tank was designed and built to serve a need. Courtesy The Owl Companies, Los Angeles, California. Photography by Joe Cosgrove.

The designer, Charles Eames, placed emphasis on functional aesthetic form and exhibited an understanding of the human anatomy in designing the lounge chair. Photograph courtesy of Charles Eames.

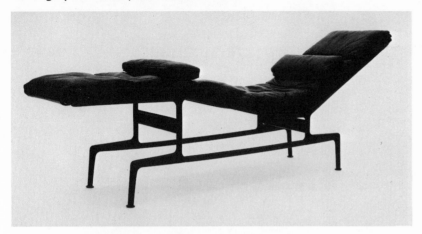

The cassette recorder emphasizes simple design concepts, easy-to-use buttons, large speaker holes, lightweight and portability, within a given cost. The recorder is functional as well as aesthetic. Photograph courtesy of Craig Corporation, Torrance, California.

The computer designer must consider what to emphasize. Concern must be given to easy-to-read numbers, buttons that do not conflict with each other during use, portability, beauty and reasonable production cost. Photograph courtesy of Craig Corporation, Torrance, California.

The design of the building emphasizes its function as a showplace for some of the world's finest art. Factors considered were location, exterior aesthetics, security, parking and accessibility. Courtesy of Los Angeles County Museum of Art.

Emphasis was on flowing, rhythmic lines in the design of the airline terminal. TWA Terminal, Kennedy International Airport, Eero Saarinen. Photograph courtesy of TWA.

"Membrane structures" and "encapsulated space" describe recent innovations in building materials, allowing reduced construction costs and giving emphasis to inventive forms on the landscape. This building serves as a multipurpose room for a college.

ARCHITECTURE

The graceful, flowing arches are given emphasis by the repetition of vertical lines that combine modern adaptations and the symbolic meaning of older systems of construction. Photograph courtesy of IBM, Seattle, Washington.

Maximum use of available space and utilization of natural light were given emphasis in the designing of the museum for viewing sculpture. Photograph courtesy of Hirshhorn Museum and Sculpture Garden, Smithsonian Institution.

SCULPTURE

The terra cotta sculpture, representing people, animals or objects, was part of a burial mound. Emphasis on cylindrical forms at the base of the sculpture was to prevent soil erosion, while the figure symbolized service to the deceased. *Haniwa Warrior.* Courtesy Seattle Art Museum, Eugene Fuller Memorial Collection.

The sculpture by Auguste Rodin emphasizes the strong diagonal line of the figure to contrast with the static placement of the minotaur, creating intense visual activity. *Minotaur*, August Rodin. Courtesy Los Angeles County Museum of Art, Gift of Mrs. Leona Cantor.

The artist, Claire Falkenstein, chose to emphasize organic and plant forms on the sculpture. When the sculpture is moved or activated by breezes, exciting audio-visual combinations result. *Flora,* Claire Falkenstein. Courtesy Blue Cross of Southern California.

Sculpture, unlike other art forms, exists in three dimensions, sharing the quality of dimension with architecture. The vertical lines of the building give emphasis to the free-form sculpture, as well as an indication of scale.

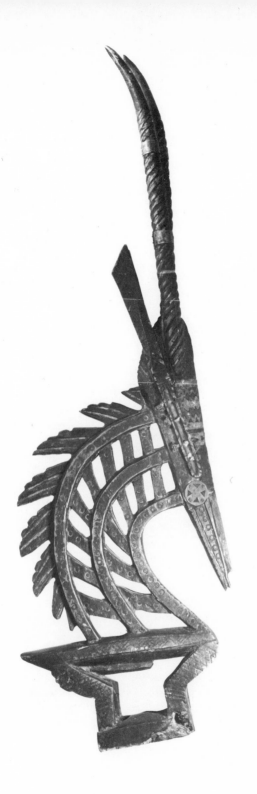

CRAFTS

The primitive craftsperson executed forms that served various rituals. The grave marker utilized small cast figures to relate various aspects of the deceased's life, while the carved antelope head gave emphasis to the dance ritual. Collection of author.

The Painters' America

The Painters'America

Rural and Urban Life, 1810-1910

Patricia Hills

Praeger Publishers   New York · Washington

In association with the Whitney Museum of American Art

To John I. H. Baur, whose scholarship in the field of American Art has been invaluable.

Frontispiece: George Luks. *The Spielers,* 1905. Oil on canvas, 36 x 26 inches. Addison Gallery of American Art, Phillips Academy, Andover, Massachusetts.

Photograph Credits

E. Irving Blomstrann, Lee Boltin, Geoffrey Clements, Bill Finney, Helga Photo Studio, Peter A. Juley & Son, Gerald Kraus, Le Bel's Studio, David Preston, Spiro, Eric Sutherland, Joseph Szaszfai, Taylor and Dull Inc., Charles Trefts, Al Wyatt

Published in the United States of America in 1974 by Praeger Publishers, Inc. 111 Fourth Avenue, New York, N.Y. 10003 in association with the Whitney Museum of American Art

Library of Congress Cataloging in Publication Data

Hills, Patricia.
    The painters' America.

    Exhibition held at the Whitney Museum of American Art, New York, Sept. 20 —Nov. 10, 1974; at the Museum of Fine Arts, Houston, Dec. 5, 1974—Jan. 19, 1975; and at the Oakland Museum, Feb. 10—Mar. 30, 1975.
    Bibliography: p.
    1. Paintings, American—Exhibitions. 2. Painting, Modern—19th century—United States. 3. Painting, Modern—20th century—United States. 4. United States in art. I. Whitney Museum of American Art, New York. II. Houston, Tex. Museum of Fine Arts. III. Oakland Museum. IV. Title.
ND210.H47   759.13   74-1721
ISBN 0-275-43700-0

Book design by Gilda Hannah Kuhlman

Printed in the United States of America

Contents

Acknowledgments

I want to thank the following who have aided me in my research and have directed me to paintings which I otherwise would not have known: Lee Baxandall, Mary Black, Houston Blume, Robin Bolton-Smith, Richard Boyle, Nicolai Cikovsky, Jr., Edward H. Dwight, Sarah Faunce, Stuart P. Feld, Linda Ferber, Lawrence A. Fleischman, Michael Frost, William H. Gerdts, Frank Goodyear, Robert C. Graham, Frederick D. Hill, John K. Howat, Stephen B. Jareckie, Agnes Jones, C. R. Jones, Louis C. Jones, Richard Koke, Cecily Langdale, Martin Leifer, Laura Luckey, Ken Lux, Maybelle Mann, George Neubert, Clyde M. Newhouse, Ross Newhouse, Kenneth M. Newman, Ellwood Parry, Dorothy Phillips, Patricia Pierce, Joseph J. Rishel, Bertha Saunders, Max Schweitzer, Kent Seavey, Darrel Sewell, Natalie Spassky, Theodore E. Stebbins, Jr., June C. Stocks, Jerome Stoker, William S. Talbot, Patricia Walker, Peter C. Welsh, Frederick Woolworth, and particularly Lloyd Goodrich for his continuing support and enthusiasm.

I want further to acknowledge Mehrnoz Mahmudian and Peninah Petruck for undertaking the enormous task of researching and writing the artists' biographies; Jacki Ochs was most helpful for typing, and Margaret Aspinwall for editing the biographies. I want also to express my appreciation to Mariann Nowack who gave me assistance at all stages of the project, and to Brenda Gilchrist, Ellyn Childs, and Cherene Holland of the Praeger staff for their unending patience and encouragement.

Both Wanda Corn and Roger Stein read early drafts of the manuscript with painstaking care. Their constructive suggestions helped me to clarify several ideas at critical points in my essay. They have my deepest gratitude.

The Painters' America
Rural and Urban Life, 1810–1910

America's finest 19th-century professional artists, aware as they were of the European artistic heritage, nevertheless mirrored their contemporary, and specifically American, experience. That experience consisted of realities and hopes, of life in its actuality, and life in its potentiality. In the previous century the portraits which dominated colonial painting delineated, and at times flattered, the pragmatic and shrewd personalities who built up the commercial strength of American ports and later rebelled against the political domination of England. Landscape painting, which developed and flourished from the beginnings of the 19th century, continually adjusted to changing attitudes—of the painters and their patrons—toward nature. The selection and conception of the American countryside by these landscapists took a variety of forms: as God's mysterious and sublime wilderness, as the pioneer's territorial and national destiny, or as the home owner's picturesque garden.

Paralleling the development of landscape painting in America was genre painting. The pictures of "everyday life," by their very definition, commented on the attitudes of painters and patrons toward the society of their time. Modifying and altering conventional European subject matter, painters gravitated toward themes of special appeal to American taste. Early in the century those themes presented optimistic and nationalistic concerns; later, the themes often shared a cosmopolitan and aesthetic viewpoint.

Studying these "paintings of everyday life" and trying to sort out and understand the roles of artistic convention, reality, and myth can bring the viewer to some rewarding insights and surprising conclusions. In many works the social references are subtle; in others the values parade explicitly and programmatically. Some artists, particularly in the early years of the century, relied heavily on historical precedent, producing pictures of organ-grinders and card players closely related to traditional genre. Other artists made pictorial records of actual events, which they exhibited as genre painting. But even those "actual events" were highly selective—often of and for a chosen audience. Generally, however, in the century from 1810 to 1910, most scenes of everyday life in America were synthetic constructions, reflecting the cultural ideals and social myths of the picture producers and picture consumers—the painters' America —rather than the actual social circumstances of the majority of the people.

The Beginnings of Genre Painting in America

Genre painting, in its traditional meaning of scenes of the lives of everyday people, first blossomed into an established branch of painting in the Netherlands in the 17th century. Adriaen Brouwer, Adriaen van Ostade, and the Flemish painter David Teniers the Younger favored depictions of "low life"—card sharpers and drunkards in taverns and kitchens. Other artists such as Gerard ter Borch, Pieter de Hooch, and Jan Vermeer preferred quiet interiors of bourgeois life. As time passed, genre painting gradually changed its character to adjust to changing circumstances and a different patronage. By the late 18th century, in England and on the Continent, sentimental, rustic genre prevailed, represented by Jean-Baptiste Greuze, Francis Wheatley, George Morland, and David Wilkie.

In 18th-century America, scenes of daily life could be found on commercial signs, banknotes, embroidery, fire screens, literary illustration, and an occasional decorative, over-mantle picture. Not until the second decade of the 19th century did genre painting emerge as a separate branch of painting in America, and then it was close to its European prototypes—emphasizing gestures, anecdotal elements, and moralizing or humorous stories.

The roots of the early-American genre painting can be found in three active 18th-century traditions: the topographical view animated with small-scale working or strolling figures; the sentimental genre painting of Greuze, Wheatley, Morland, and, later, Wilkie; and the heritage of political and social satire represented by William Hogarth, James Gillray, Thomas Rowlandson, and George Cruikshank.

In New York at the turn of the 18th century, Francis Guy painted a number of topographical scenes of Brooklyn and New York village life. In *Winter Scene in Brooklyn* of about 1817–20 Guy rendered the existing buildings with precise exactness (*Ill. 1*). In Philadelphia the engraver William Russell Birch, with the help of his son Thomas, issued a number of *Views of Philadelphia* in 1800.[1] Influenced by these topographical scenes of Birch and others, John Lewis

Krimmel painted *View of Centre Square, on the 4th of July,* about 1810–12 (*Ill. 2*). The painting represents a variety of city types posed against a backdrop of Philadelphia scenery, including the Pump House designed by Benjamin Henry Latrobe and William Rush's statue *Water Nymph and Bittern.* When the painting was exhibited at the Second Annual Exhibition of the Society of Artists of the United States in 1812, one reviewer singled out Krimmel's painting for praise:

> There are few people (if any) who visit the Academy, who are not perfectly acquainted with the scene of which this is so familiar and pleasing a representation. It is truly *Hogarthian,* and full of meaning, the figures are amply varied, and the character highly diversified. The artist has proved himself no common observer of the tragicomical events of life that are daily and hourly passing before us.[2]

Krimmel had studied the prints of the English and European genre painters, and he came to be known as "the American Hogarth."

As strong an influence as Hogarth was David Wilkie. In 1813 Krimmel submitted a copy after Wilkie's *The Blind Fiddler (Ill. 5)* to the Third Annual Exhibition of the Columbian Society of Artists and the Pennsylvania Academy of the Fine Arts. He made other copies after Wilkie, which were also admired by his contemporaries.

A writer for *The Analectic Magazine* of February, 1820, describing an engraving after Krimmel's *Country Wedding (Ill. 3)* was well aware of both the tradition of genre and its contemporary European practitioners:

> [Krimmel] has painted many pictures in which the style of Wilkie—so much admired in England—and Gerard Dow [*sic*] so much celebrated of yore—is most successfully followed. He avoids the broad humor of the Flemish school as much as possible, as not congenial to the refinement of modern taste, and aims rather at a true portraiture of nature in real, rustic life.

1. Francis Guy. *Winter Scene in Brooklyn*, c. 1817–20. Oil on canvas, 58¾ x 75 inches. The Brooklyn Museum. Gift of the Brooklyn Institute.

2. John Lewis Krimmel. *View of Centre Square, on the 4th of July,* c. 1810–12. Oil on canvas, 23 x 29 inches. Pennsylvania Academy of the Fine Arts, Philadelphia. Academy Purchase, 1845.

3

3. John Lewis Krimmel. *Country Wedding*, c. 1819. Oil on canvas, 16¾ x 22½ inches. Pennsylvania Academy of the Fine Arts, Philadelphia. Presented by Paul Beck, 1842.

4. Jean-Baptiste Greuze. *The Village Bride*, Salon of 1761. Oil on canvas. Photograph courtesy of Les Musées Nationaux, Paris.

In the picture here presented he has delineated a scene of no rare occurrence in the dwellings of our native yeomenry.[3]

European artistic formulas for the form and content are relied upon. The sentimental subject of two lovers being married by the village priest recalls *The Village Bride* by the 18th-century French artist Jean-Baptiste Greuze (*Ill. 4*). The composition follows the tradition of late 18th-century interiors. Within the shallow, bilaterally symmetrical space, competing activities take place with guests entering, children squabbling, and a solemn, elderly gentleman performing the marriage rites. The faces of the figures have stock neoclassic features with straight noses, full lips, and rounded chins; their expressions vary only slightly. The anecdotal meaning is conveyed by gestures and supplemental motifs, such as the framed picture entitled "Mariage" [*sic*] above the mantle and the cooing doves above the betrothed couple.

Krimmel's works—exhibited often in Philadelphia before his early death in 1821—were bought by the important collectors of his time and were popularized through engravings and lithographs. The prints became an important source of motifs and style to the next generation of genre painters. William Sidney Mount's *Rustic Dance After a Sleigh Ride* of 1830, with its black fiddler and dancing couple, is similar in composition, motifs, and mood to the Childs and Lehman lithograph *Dance in a Country Tavern* after Krimmel's *Country Frolic and Dance*[4] (*Ills. 6, 7*). The anonymous *The Return from Town* (*Ill. 8*) was painted after a John Sartain engraving of a work by Krimmel.

Itinerant musicians remained a popular subject to Americans throughout the 19th century, but peddlers seemed to have a particular and special meaning. While the fiddler was often a black, as in the print after Krimmel *Dance in a Country Tavern*, the peddler was invariably a white man. In Asher Brown Durand's *The Peddler Displaying His Wares* of 1836 the peddler of trinkets is an elderly but animated man (*Ill. 9*). Scenes of peddlers would appeal to collectors and art patrons such as Luman Reed. Reed was engaged in marketing as an affluent wholesale grocer, and it was he who bought this painting by Durand. The motif of the black man appearing peripherally to the scene—either at a door behind or at the side of the central activity—occurs frequently in pre-Civil War genre painting. The black man added a touch of regional picturesqueness, identifying the scene as "American."

Later the peddler became more youthful and virile. In Francis William Edmonds's *The Image Peddler* of 1844—a painting owned and exhibited by the New York Gallery of Fine Arts in the 1850s—the peddler became the analogue to the real-life Yankee entrepreneur (*Ill. 10*). Although upward social mobility was never as easy as the advocates of "Jacksonian democracy" would have us believe, nevertheless in the pre-Civil War years an enterprising white male could amass a fortune through a series of clever dealings. And success was appealing to both artist and patron. Moreover, artists who traveled from town to village in search of customers must have identified with the peddler. The salesman of the small plaster Washington head in Edmonds's painting *The Image Peddler* may have been the maker of the images. In Charles Bird King's *The Itinerant Artist* of about 1825–30, the artist has unpacked his portable easel, paints, and brushes (very much as the peddler would), and is commencing the portrait of the lady of the rustic house (*Ill. 12*).

As far as is known, William Sidney Mount never painted a picture of an itinerant artist, but he certainly considered adopting the style of life of the transient artist. In a diary entry from Stony Brook, of November 17, 1852, he considered the possibility:

> Perhaps it would be greatly to my interest to travel with my waggon [*sic*] and paint pictures and occasionally a portrait to keep up a large style of handling. I could find rooms with two windows in every village and city— There would be a novelty in the enterprise. I must think of it—better be moving than rusting out in one place.[5]

Mount's 1838 painting *The Painter's Triumph* is his comment on the role and status of the artist in America (*Ill. 13*). In a relatively uncluttered studio a

5. David Wilkie. *The Blind Fiddler*, 1806. Oil on panel, 22¾ x 31¼ inches. The Trustees of The Tate Gallery, London.

6. Childs and Lehman. *Dance in a Country Tavern*, after John Lewis Krimmel, c. 1833–36. Hand-colored lithograph, 7⅞ x 10⅞ inches (composition). Photograph courtesy of The Old Print Shop, New York.

7. William Sidney Mount. *Rustic Dance After a Sleigh Ride*, 1830. Oil on canvas, 22 x 27¼ inches. Museum of Fine Arts, Boston. M. and M, Karolik Collection.

8. Unknown artist. *The Return from Town*, after a John Sartain engraving of a painting by John Lewis Krimmel, 1840s. Oil on canvas, 18 x 26 inches. New York State Historical Association, Cooperstown.

9. Asher Brown Durand. *The Peddler Displaying His Wares* (1836). Oil on canvas,
24 x 34 inches. The New-York Historical Society, New York.

10. Francis William Edmonds. *The Image Peddler* (1844). Oil on canvas, 33 x 42 inches. The New-York Historical Society, New York.

11. John Whetten Ehninger. *Yankee Peddler,* 1853. Oil on canvas, 25¾ x 32½ inches. The Newark Museum, Newark, New Jersey.

12. Charles Bird King. *The Itinerant Artist,* c. 1825–30. Oil on canvas, 44¾ x 57 inches. New York State Historical Association, Cooperstown.

13. William Sidney Mount. *The Painter's Triumph,* 1838. Oil on wood, 19½ x 23½ inches. Pennsylvania Academy of the Fine Arts, Philadelphia. Henry C. Carey Collection, 1879.

painter triumphantly exhibits his work in progress to a local farmer.[6] The painter stands stage center in a heroic, classical pose, better dressed than his rustic companion but grateful for his admiration. As a reference to the painter's artistic heritage, a maul-stick leaning against the back wall points to a drawing of the head of the Apollo Belvedere. The farmer may understand the artistic product, but the face of the Apollo turns grimly away from this scene of excessive enthusiasm. In spite of such subtle touches, the painting declared the popularly held notion that American painters, as democrats, courted the appreciation of all the citizenry, and it is no coincidence that the work was bought by E. L. Carey of Philadelphia, publisher of *The Gift,* one of the popular Christmas annuals that patronized writers of "American" stories and painters of "American" scenes.

In fact, even today, Mount's declaration "Never paint for the few, but for the many" is marshaled as evidence of his egalitarian spirit. The quotation is lifted from his notes regarding his patrons and the full passage is worth quoting: "Paint pictures that will take with the public, in other words, never paint for the few, but for the many— Some artists remain in the corner by not observing the above."[7]

To Mount, "the public" were those who bought his pictures. Whereas many early 19th-century artists aspired to social prestige—which was not the case with Mount—he nevertheless placed a high priority on the accolades of connoisseurs and their assured patronage. In 1850 he remarked in his diary: "I must paint up my commissions without delay, that alone will occupy all my day time. I must not lose sight of my real friends, those who give me orders."[8]

In other words, Mount was no different from any other professional artist who earned his living through his art; to sell his work, he had to tailor it to the demands of those who would pay.[9]

David Claypool Johnston's *The Artist and the Tyro (Ill. 14)* contrasts humorously with Mount's *The Painter's Triumph.* A sometime actor, Johnston was called "the American Cruikshank" because of his satirical sketches. In the Johnston painting, the viewer sees the artist, the model, and the picture. The painted image represents the scowling boy-soldier standing at attention on the flag of the Confederate States of America, with his ineffectual toy popgun by his side. On the background wall hangs a heroic painting of soldiers with real weapons charging into battle with the Union flag waving high. The portraits of the women, representing family, and the portrait of George Washington, symbolizing patriotism, look on approvingly.

Johnston and a number of other early 19th-century artists explored the tradition of satirical and humorous genre passed along by Hogarth, Gillray, Rowlandson, and Cruikshank, which found a natural outlet in illustrations of literary works. Washington Allston's *The Poor Author and the Rich Bookseller* of 1811 with its rotund, complacent bookseller dismissing the thin, pinched, and worried author, literally swept aside, suggests a literary reference[10] *(Ill. 15)*.

Allston was a close friend of Washington Irving, and he designed several illustrations for Irving's *Knickerbocker's History of New York,* a humorous, historical account of New Netherlands, and for Irving's *The Legend of Sleepy Hollow* and *Rip Van Winkle,* tales dealing with the customs and folklore of the Hudson River Valley under the Dutch patroons. Subjects and themes from Irving's satirical but distinctly regional stories inspired a generation of artists, most notably John Quidor, Henry Inman, Albertus D. O. Browere, and F. O. C. Darley[11] *(Ills. 16, 17)*.

Many traveling Europeans, themselves familiar with a polished aristocracy, viewed life in Jacksonian America as epitomizing vulgarity and uncouth manners,[12] and some patrons obviously delighted in paintings which represented our rude, democratic manners. James Goodwyn Clonney's *Politicians in a Country Bar* of 1844 depicts the type of local character who would have an influence on local affairs *(Ill. 18)*. One animated debator lifts his foot to make a point,* while the other pulls on his chair. A black man leans against the door frame—a silent witness, whose faint shadow barely reaches the central activity. A woman standing in the kitchen doorway is also peripheral to the proceedings. Even in this hu-

*No. He is sitting on table.

14. David Claypool Johnston. *The Artist and the Tyro,* c. 1863. Oil on canvas, 17 x 14 inches. Private collection, New York.

15. Washington Allston. *The Poor Author and the Rich Bookseller* (1811). Oil on canvas, 31 x 28 inches. Museum of Fine Arts, Boston. Bequest of Charles Sprague Sargent.

16. John Quidor. *The Return of Rip Van Winkle*, 1829. Oil on canvas, 39¾ x 49¾ inches. National Gallery of Art, Washington, D.C. Andrew Mellon Collection, 1942.

17. Henry Inman. *Dismissal of School on an October Afternoon*, 1845. Oil on canvas, 26 x
36 inches. Museum of Fine Arts, Boston. M. and M. Karolik Collection.

morous rendition, the real political and social status of women and blacks—their exclusion from real decision-making—is made clear.

Young women were rarely rendered humorously; however, older women, such as the proprietress in Albertus D. O. Browere's *Mrs. McCormick's General Store* of 1844, could become the butt of a joke (*Ill. 19*). Mrs. McCormick rushes out of her store to seize a young mischief-maker. His companion thumbs his nose, while another steals a piece of fruit.

In John Carlin's *After a Long Cruise* of 1857, sailors on leave from their ship behave like funny, naughty boys (*Colorplate 2*). Intended to be humorous, their drunken antics include knocking over a peanut-and-apple vendor's stand and reaching amorously toward a strolling young black woman. At the side two boys take advantage of the confusion by grabbing at pieces of fruit that have fallen to the street. Resourcefulness was a virtue and the young boys' actions would have seemed most enterprising.

The humor in Johnston's *Wide Awake—Sound Asleep* resides in its punning on illusion and reality (*Ill. 20*). The practical joker paints a grinning face on the bald posterior of the sleeping man's head. To

18. James Goodwyn Clonney. *Politicians in a Country Bar*, 1844. Oil on canvas, 17⅛ x 21⅛ inches. New York State Historical Association, Cooperstown.

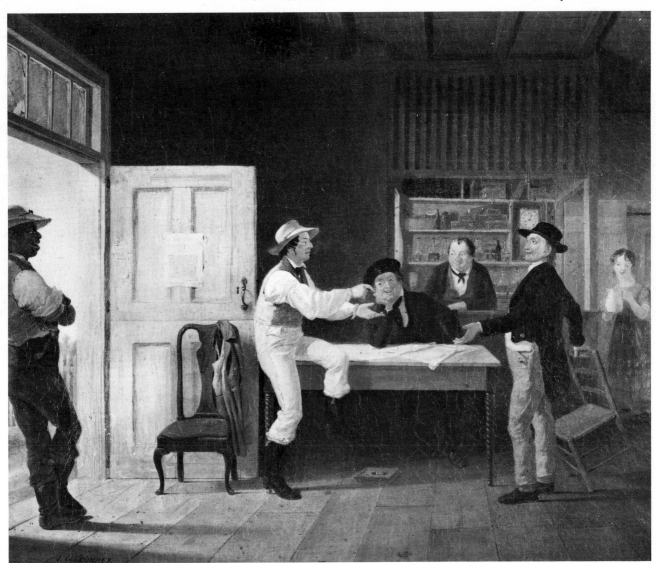

16

Colorplate 1. John Lewis Krimmel. *Country Tavern, Arrival of the Post with News of Peace,* c. 1814–15. Oil on canvas, 16⅞ x 22½ inches. The Toledo Museum of Art, Toledo, Ohio. Gift of Florence Scott Libbey, 1954.

Colorplate 2. John Carlin. *After a Long Cruise (Salts Ashore)*, 1857. Oil on canvas, 20 x 30 inches. The Metropolitan Museum of Art, New York. Purchase, 1949, Maria DeWitt Jesup Fund.

19. Albertus D. O. Browere. *Mrs. Mc-Cormick's General Store* (1844). Oil on canvas, 20½ x 25 inches. New York State Historical Association, Cooperstown.

20. David Claypool Johnston. *Wide Awake—Sound Asleep,* c. 1845. Oil on canvas, 21¾ x 17⅝ inches. Collection of the Honorable and Mrs. H. John Heinz III, Washington, D.C.

21. William Sidney Mount. *Farmers Nooning*, 1836. Oil on canvas, 20 x 24 inches. Suffolk Museum & Carriage House, Stony Brook, Long Island, New York. Melville Collection.

the viewer of the picture, the painted face is the image he sees, and thus the only face he knows.

Practical jokes played on sleepers often involved a black man as the victim. Young boys tickle the nose of a sleeping black man in Mount's *Farmers Nooning* of 1836 (*Ill. 21*). After its exhibition at the National Academy of Design in 1837 and distribution as a print by the American Art-Union in 1843, the motif became part of the vocabulary of painters of the time. In James Clonney's *Waking Up* of 1851, malevolent, young white boys tease a black fisherman (*Ill. 22*). The Clonney painting was exhibited at the National Academy of Design in 1851.

Mount himself considered the subject again. In a diary entry dated September 15, 1850, he listed the commissions he was working on for his patron, the lithograph publisher, William Schaus. Mount notes: "One picture cabinet size—negro asleep in a barn—while a little boy is endeavoring to tickel [*sic*] the negro's ear, another little boy is tickling his foot."[13]

The subject received even broader circulation with the Currier & Ives 1868 lithograph *Holidays in the Country: Troublesome Flies (Ill. 23)*. Again, a black man lies sleeping while young white boys swarm about him. At a time when the collective strength of black men loomed as a potential to be reckoned

22. James Goodwyn Clonney. *Waking Up*, 1851. Oil on canvas, 27 x 22 inches. Museum of Fine Arts, Boston. M. and M. Karolik Collection.

23. Currier & Ives. *Holidays in the Country: Troublesome Flies*, 1868. Hand-colored lithograph, 15⅛ x 23⅛ inches (composition). Photograph courtesy of The Old Print Shop, New York.

21

24. William Sidney Mount. *Loss and Gain,* 1847. Oil on canvas, 24 x 20 inches. Suffolk Museum & Carriage House, Stony Brook, Long Island, New York. Melville Collection.

with, his reduction to an impotent plaything of children must have been a reassuring motif. Through the distribution of popular prints, moreover, the image of powerlessness received wide currency.

In humorous genre, the learned weaknesses and foibles of characters were held up to ridicule; often the moralizing lessons were obvious. Both Francis William Edmonds's *Facing the Enemy* of about 1845 and William Sidney Mount's *Loss and Gain* of 1847 depict the temptations and frustrations that beset old men (*Ills. 24, 25*). In the Edmonds painting, the old man sits in a chair between his carpenter's tools and the jug placed on the windowsill. With his back to the symbols of honest and respectable work, he stares at the jug, which represents the freedom from responsibilities but also social disgrace. In Mount's *Loss and Gain,* the jug has spilled on the ground; the old man's loss is really his gain.

As mid-century approached, genre painting lost many of its overtly humorous aspects. The vulgarity of traditional genre had no appeal to an art audience which began to imbibe the moralism and idealism of John Ruskin.[14] The times dictated that art must edify and uplift its audience. This idealism was inextricably bound to the particular nationalism of the times.

25. Francis William Edmonds. *Facing the Enemy* (1845). Oil on board, 10½ x 9 inches. Private collection, New York.

The Reflection of Nationalism in Art

The late 18th and 19th centuries saw the formation and reorganization of several European nations where nationalism—pride in one's country, reverence for her past, and optimism for her future—was encouraged. What characterized American nationalism in the Jacksonian era and for several decades following was the special glorification, among the politicians and writers, of the rural worker and the pioneer.[15] Eventually our nationalism tended to emphasize present and future greatness rather than the mythic past and military glories.

During the second quarter of the 19th century, writers and poets mirrored the political nationalism in their preoccupations with creating an indigenous literature—a literature describing the local customs of Americans. Washington Irving, one of our first great writers, exploited the potential of colonial history and legends to shape a literature. James Fenimore Cooper followed in 1824 with the publication of *The Pioneers,* the first of his Leatherstocking Tales. Ralph Waldo Emerson and Henry Wadsworth Longfellow also urged their countrymen to turn toward American subjects. Emerson advised poets and artists to celebrate ordinary subject matter in his Phi Beta Kappa address delivered at Harvard College on August 31, 1837:

> The literature of the poor, the feelings of the child, the philosophy of the street, the meaning of household life, are the topics of the time. It is a great stride. It is a sign . . . of new vigor . . . . I ask not for the great, the remote, the romantic; what is doing in Italy or Arabia; what is Greek art, or Provençal minstrelsy; I embrace the common, I explore and sit at the feet of the familiar, the low. . . . The meal in the firkin; the milk in the pan; the ballad in the street; the news of the boat; the glance of the eye.[16]

And in 1842 he exhorted:

> Our logrolling, our stumps, and their politics, our fisheries, our Negroes and Indians, our boats . . . the northern trade, the southern planting, the western clearing, Oregon and Texas, are yet unsung. Yet America is a poem in our eyes: its ample geography dazzles the imagination.[17]

Years later Walt Whitman made the broadest appeal when he declared in his 1855 preface to *Leaves of Grass* his intention to interpret the present national character and the future national destiny.[18]

The American gift books that emerged during the 1820s, 1830s, and 1840s as rivals to their English prototypes, reflected this nationalism at the most popular level. Their publishers consistently employed American writers and designers to delineate "American" local scenes. An editorial, which appeared in *The Garland* in 1830, deserves to be quoted at length as representative of the emerging attitudes in popular literature:

> Until within a short period, the few men who were distinguished in this country either in polite literature or the arts were mere pupils of the English schools . . . . Similar remarks would also apply to American painters. Until within a few years they seldom condescended to spoil their canvases with an American landscape or a scene from Yankee history. We are happy to observe that a new era of literature and the arts has dawned upon our country . . . . Our own painters, too, have at length discovered the beauty with which nature is adorned in this western world, and the moral interest which attaches to the pages of its history. Painting, poetry, and romance, even of a national and historical character, are imagined to be childish trifles by many, and by many others to be pernicious instruments of folly and dissipation. We regard them in a very different light. We believe them to be powerful auxiliaries to the formation of national character—calculated in their nature to elevate and refine society, and to cherish and confirm one of the best sentiments of the human breast—love of country.[19]

The publishers of *The Gift,* in 1843, pronounced their book "in every respect an American work. The contributions are by American authors—the illustrations by American artists."[20] So strong was the preference for indigenous subject matter that a few gift books and periodicals, such as the sporting journal

Spirit of the Times in 1847, discontinued foreign articles in favor of "articles truly American . . . presenting the peculiar characteristics of, and illustrating scenes and incidents throughout 'the Universal Yankee nation.'"[21]

The nationalism that pervaded the country in the late 1830s, 1840s, and early 1850s—of which literary and artistic nationalism was but a symptom—was in part a reaction to the great influx of immigrants during the period. Samuel F. B. Morse wrote a tract in 1835, *Imminent Dangers to the Free Institutions of the United States Through Foreign Immigration, and the Present State of the Naturalization Laws.* Morse and the Reverend Lyman Beecher were leaders in the "Know-Nothing" movement, which advocated the exclusion of all but native Americans from political office and a twenty-five-year residence requirement for citizenship.

Dissemination of Art Through the Art Unions

From the time of its organization in 1826, the National Academy of Design held annual exhibitions of the works of its members. In 1844 the New York Art Gallery also exhibited paintings. In Philadelphia and Boston annual exhibitions were held at the Pennsylvania Academy of the Fine Arts and the Boston Athenaeum from the early years of the century. However, these art organizations were not vehicles for the sale and distribution of paintings. That role fell to the art unions, which sprang up in the 1840s and 1850s. The aim of the art unions was to elevate the taste of all Americans and to create a broad-based market for the sale of fine art. The most influential was the American Art-Union, founded in 1838 in New York City as the Apollo Association. Its purpose, as set forth in its charter, was unabashedly nationalistic:

> The American Art-Union, in the city of New York, was incorporated . . . for the PROMOTION OF THE FINE ARTS IN THE UNITED STATES. It is managed by gentlemen who are chosen annually to be members, and receive no

compensation. To accomplish A TRULY NATIONAL OBJECT, uniting great public good with private gratification at small individual expense, in a manner best suited to the situation and institutions of our country, and the wants, habits, and tastes of our people, the Committee have adopted the following PLAN.[22]

The "PLAN" outlined the benefits of membership. Members, upon payment of five-dollar annual dues, were entitled to receive each year one or two engravings that had been commissioned by the Union and an illustrated periodical, and were eligible to receive paintings in the annual lottery. The American Art-Union had an active life of about twelve years; in 1849, its year of greatest membership, it distributed 1,010 works among 18,960 subscribers. The artists supported by the Union enjoyed a patronage that hardly existed before. And the Union wholeheartedly encouraged specifically American scenes. In 1843 the Union proudly announced that: "The largest part of the works . . . [was] illustrative of American scenery and American manners. The Committee would be happy to distribute none others."[23]

The *Bulletin of the American Art-Union* repeatedly singled out paintings celebrating American history and the American scene. The remarks in an issue of the *Bulletin* of 1849 regarding a watercolor sketch of an incident in the life of Peter Stuyvesant by John Whetten Ehninger seem typical of the editors' enthusiasm: "It will be a very effective picture, and it is gratifying to see that he will make the first fruit of his foreign studies an illustration of the history of his native city."[24]

The works which the Union chose to engrave influenced many young artists outside New York. Although there were some historical paintings by John B. White, John Vanderlyn, Emanuel Leutze, and others, and ideal subjects by Daniel Huntington and Thomas Cole, the majority of the prints were of genre subjects.

"National" subjects often meant depictions of unique, regional customs. In Alvan T. Fisher's *The Corn Husking Frolic* of 1828–29, the country lad holds up a red ear of corn which, according to New

26. Alvan T. Fisher. *The Corn Husking Frolic*, 1828–29. Oil on panel, 27¾ x 24¼ inches. Museum of Fine Arts, Boston. M. and M. Karolik Collection.

England tradition, entitles him to a kiss from the nearest young woman (*Ill. 26*). William Sidney Mount's *Raffling for the Goose* of 1837 and *Ringing the Pig* of 1842 represent other typically "American" farm rituals of Long Island (*Ills. 27, 28*).

The usual interpretation of Mount's paintings as representing the "classless" society of the Jacksonian era is modified by a close examination of many of his canvases. In *Raffling for the Goose* the two figures on the right, obviously of a higher social status as indicated by their clothes and beaver hunting caps, stand further away than the local farmers from the denuded goose lying on the makeshift table. Stratification by class was as pronounced as in European countries; the difference was that in America there was hope of the possibilities of equality. After all, the Constitution had declared "All men are created equal."[25]

The egalitarian reputation of the era must be seriously questioned when one considers the place of women and blacks (both free and slave) in the society. Written records of the laws, statistics, and historical reports give evidence of the actual conditions for most people, but literature and art mirrored the assumptions and attitudes. Mount's *Dance of the Haymakers* of 1845 and his *The Power of Music* of 1847 both represent barn scenes, and, in each, white folks make music inside the barn while a black stands outside, unobserved by the others (*Ills. 29, 30*). The title *The Power of Music*, mollifies the black man's exclusion; the painting becomes a 19th-century visualization of the "separate but equal" philosophy of race relations. In other words, although the black man is outside and not allowed to participate in white society, the appreciation of music is universal. To the white viewers of Mount's painting, the black man's "spiritual equality" made up for the other inequalities.

27. William Sidney Mount. *Ringing the Pig* (1842). Oil on canvas, 25 x 30 inches. New York State Historical Association, Cooperstown.

28. William Sidney Mount. *Raffling for the Goose,* 1837. Oil on wood, 17 x 23⅛ inches. The Metropolitan Museum of Art, New York. Gift of John D. Crimmins, 1897.

29. William Sidney Mount. *The Power of Music*, 1847. Oil on canvas, 17 x 21 inches. The Century Association, New York.

30. William Sidney Mount. *Dance of the Haymakers*, 1845. Oil on canvas, 25 x 30 inches. Suffolk Museum & Carriage House, Stony Brook, Long Island, New York. Melville Collection.

American farm activities and regional enterprises involving groups of farmers and their families were represented in scenes of haying, cornhusking, cider making, maple-sugar camps, and turkey shoots. William Sidney Mount's *Cider Making* of 1841, William T. Carlton's *Cider Mill* of about 1855, and Jerome B. Thompson's *Apple Gathering* of 1856 are bucolic visions of the communal effort of harvesting and pressing the apples (*Ills. 31, 32; Colorplate 3*). George Henry Durrie's *Cider Making in the Country* of 1863 with its mill nestled among the trees visualizes the compatibility of the rural industry with nature (*Ill. 33*). Many such scenes were lithographed by the leading publishing firms. Durrie specialized in farm scenes for Currier & Ives, which distributed a print of another version, *Autumn in New England: Cider Making,* in 1866. Otis A. Bullard, a contemporary of Mount, painted *Loading Hay* in 1846, adding a touch of sentimental humor by including a dog stalking a mouse hidden in the hay (*Ill. 34*). Barn scenes were not necessarily specific to a particular region, but they sustained a continued popularity. Durrie's *Farmyard in Winter, Selling Corn* of 1852 represents commercial transactions in a barn in wintertime (*Ill. 35*). Eastman Johnson filled the demand by painting *Corn Husking* in 1860 (*Ill. 36*), a scene engraved and distributed by Currier & Ives.

A regional activity popular with artists was the spring maple-sugar harvest in the Northeastern woods. Sociability and merrymaking, as well as work, characterized the sugar camp. In 1845 Tompkins Harrison Matteson painted *Sugaring Off,* a scene of city people visiting rustics in a maple-sugar camp (*Ill. 37*). Matteson's winter idyll contains an amusing rustic blowing on a steaming spoonful of syrup surrounded by dapper gentlemen and enamel-skinned, doll-like ladies. In 1856 Nathaniel Currier distributed a large folio print of Arthur Fitzwilliam Tait's *American Forest Scene—Maple Sugaring;* in 1872 Currier & Ives issued *Maple Sugaring: Early Spring in the Northern Woods.* In both prints the figures are all from the same rural milieu, rather than contrasting country bumpkins and city sophisticates.

Eastman Johnson followed Tait's lead by eliminating class distinctions between the working participants and the spectators. In Johnson's *Sugaring Off,* the artist did not attempt to paint a single realistic event, but rather a synthesis of typical "sugaring off" activities (*Ill. 38*). The various groupings give the viewer a flavor of the joyousness of this New England vernal celebration which followed weeks of work and months of cold winter.

Johnson, and also John Ehninger, gave rural workers a dignity demanded by the idealism and nationalism of the time. In 1857 a writer for the *Cosmopolitan Art Journal,* in an article entitled "American Painters: Their Errors as Regards Nationality," went so far as to equate the "noble" purpose of art with patriotism:

> Akin with every other utilitarian science, painting has its instructive mission, ever varying as

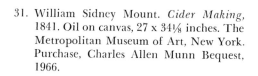

31. William Sidney Mount. *Cider Making,* 1841. Oil on canvas, 27 x 34⅛ inches. The Metropolitan Museum of Art, New York. Purchase, Charles Allen Munn Bequest, 1966.

32. William T. Carlton. *Cider Mill*, c. 1855. Oil on canvas, 29 x 36 inches. New York State Historical Association, Cooperstown.

33. George Henry Durrie. *Cider Making in the Country*, 1863. Oil on canvas, 35⅜ by 54 inches. New York State Historical Association, Cooperstown.

34. Otis A. Bullard. *Loading Hay,* 1846. Oil on canvas, 27 x 38¼ inches. Collection of Mr. and Mrs. Lewis R. Holding, Raleigh, North Carolina. Photograph courtesy of Newhouse Galleries, New York.

35. George Henry Durrie. *Farmyard in Winter, Selling Corn,* 1852. Oil on panel, 19½ x 24 inches. Shelburne Museum, Inc., Shelburne, Vermont.

36. Eastman Johnson. *Corn Husking,* 1860. Oil on canvas, 26 x 30 inches. Everson Museum of Art, Syracuse, New York.

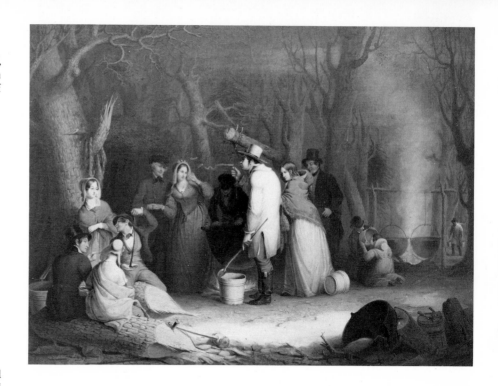

37. Tompkins Harrison Matteson. *Sugaring Off*, 1845. Oil on canvas, 30¼ x 41½ inches. Museum of Art, Carnegie Institute, Pittsburgh. Bequest of Miss Rosalie Spang.

38. Eastman Johnson. *Sugaring Off*, c. 1861–66. Oil on canvas, 34 x 54¼ inches. Collection of Mr. and Mrs. James W. Titelman.

the characteristics of the people change from progress of civilization. To be merely decorative, art fails of its object in invention; for it possesses a nobler purpose, which may be justly defined as the conservation of patriotism. As language keeps alive the fire of nationality, so should painting embalm the genius of a country by preserving memory of familiar scenes, or by transmitting to posterity reminiscences of actions, deeds or manners.[26]

Preserving the memory of familiar scenes became the tacit mission of Johnson and others, who continued to paint rural New England life—quaint old men and old-fashioned crafts—long after the end of the Civil War when the attention of Americans had turned to the cities and modern industry. Even in their own day the paintings were frankly nostalgic.[27] Henry T. Tuckerman commented in 1867 on Johnson's paintings:

> One of the latest subjects which have occupied his [Johnson's] pencil is drawn from his own childhood's reminiscences of the scenes amid which he was born. In Maine, of old, no rustic festival equalled [sic] in merriment and local interest the "boiling-day" in the sugar camp. The woods of maple glow with fire; picturesque groups of farmers and gudewives, and maidens and children animate the forest; a gossip lays down the law here; a political quidnunc comments on a stale newspaper there; old people smoke pipes on a mossy bank; young ones whisper love by the thicket. There is usually a fiddler, an ancient negro, and an improvised feast; and all these elements, with the woods for a background, and characteristic dresses, faces and groups, combine to form rare materials for a scene quite peculiar to this country; yet becoming more rare and less picturesque as locomotive facilities reduce costume, dress, speech, and even faces, to monotonous uniformity.[28]

Nostalgia—reminiscences of "the good old days"— became a hedge against the unknown future, against the upset of the old social structures which the Civil War had engendered. In 1867 a divided nation could be reunited by promoting nationalism, and regional American scenes were reminders of our shared experiences and of our differences from Europe.

In the country, and of course on the frontier, the gun was a standard piece of equipment. Men used rifles as protection against attacking Indians and white bandits. In their leisure time, farmers and frontiersmen turned to shooting contests as a form of relaxation and sport. George Caleb Bingham, raised on the frontier, painted *Shooting for the Beef* in 1850 (*Colorplate 4*). Charles Deas and Tompkins Matteson painted the scene of the turkey shooting competition in James Fenimore Cooper's *The Pioneers*.[29] As late as 1879, John Ehninger painted *Turkey Shoot*, a panoramic sweep of rural New Englanders on a wintry day contesting for the Thanksgiving turkey (*Ill. 39*).

Scenes showing children handling weapons seem to be particular to American art in the 19th century. In reality the duties of many young farm boys included killing rodents and other small animals dangerous to crops, as in John G. Chapman's *Drawing a Bead on a Woodchuck* of about 1841 (*Ill. 40*). In William Holbrook Beard's *Stalking Prairie Chicken* of 1872, nature is about to seek revenge on the boy-hunter as the bear noses his way into the scene, unknown to the creeping boy[30] (*Ill. 42*). In John George Brown's *A Sure Shot* of about 1875, the young girl stands behind the boy intent on the action of the rifle (*Ill. 41*). In retrospect it seems that the painter viewed the boy as a covert metaphor for the innocence and youth of America and viewed the gun as symbolic of the white, man-child's power over his environment.

The most popular sporting paintings before the Civil War, those which received a wide circulation through lithographs and engravings, featured ordinary scouts and farmers in the wilds of nature—in the woods or in the marsh. William Tylee Ranney's *On the Wing* of 1850 shows the concentration of the hunter and the tenseness of the boy and the dog waiting in the marsh (*Ill. 43*). Arthur Fitzwilliam

Colorplate 3. Jerome B. Thompson. *Apple Gathering,* 1856. Oil on canvas, 40½ x 50 inches. The Brooklyn Museum. Dick S. Ramsay Fund and Bequest of Laura L. Barnes.

Colorplate 4. George Caleb Bingham. *Shooting for the Beef,* 1850. Oil on canvas, 33½ x 49¼ inches. The Brooklyn Museum. Dick S. Ramsay Fund.

39. John Whetten Ehninger. *Turkey Shoot,*
1879. Oil on canvas, 25 x 43½ inches.
Museum of Fine Arts, Boston. M. and M.
Karolik Collection.

40. John G. Chapman. *Drawing a Bead on
a Woodchuck,* c. 1841. Oil on canvas,
16¼ x 21½ inches. The Butler Institute
of American Art, Youngstown, Ohio.

41. John George Brown. *A Sure Shot,* c. 1875. Oil on canvas, 21⅛ x 15 inches. The Brooklyn Museum. Dick S. Ramsay Fund.

42. William Holbrook Beard. *Stalking Prairie Chicken*, 1872. Oil on canvas, 20 x 16 inches. Trinity College, Hartford, Connecticut. The George F. McMurray Collection.

43. William Tylee Ranney. *On the Wing*, 1850. Oil on canvas, 29¾ x 44¾ inches. Kimbell Art Museum, Fort Worth.

44. Arthur Fitzwilliam Tait. *A Good Chance*, 1862. Oil on canvas, 20⅛ x 30⅛ inches. Yale University Art Gallery, New Haven. The Whitney Collections of Sporting Art, given in memory of Harry Payne Whitney and Payne Whitney by Francis P. Garvan.

45. Arthur Fitzwilliam Tait. *Mink Trapping in Northern New York*, 1862. Oil on canvas, 20½ x 30½ inches. Munson-Williams-Proctor Institute, Utica, New York.

Tait's *A Good Chance* of 1862 is set against the virgin remoteness of the Northern woods (*Ill. 44*). Tait was one of the most popular of the Currier & Ives artists of sporting subjects. His *Mink Trapping in Northern New York* of the same year represents a commercial wilderness activity, since trapping was a source of income for farmers in the winter (*Ill. 45*). Whereas the European sporting picture was consciously aristocratic, representing ladies, gentlemen, and their servants, the American product emphasized the importance of fishing and hunting to the frontiersman, the farmer, young boys, and occasionally a black.

Paintings of Town and Village Life

Before the Civil War artists also depicted village and city life. At times the rivalry of city and country life became the theme of a painting, as in William Sidney Mount's *The Sportsman's Last Visit* of 1835 and Francis William Edmonds's *The City and the Country Beaux* of 1840 (*Ills. 46, 47*). In the Mount version, the sportsman has come to call, only to discover his beloved being wooed by a soberly dressed gentleman visitor. The title of the painting gives a clue to the situation. In Edmonds's painting, the country suitor is a catalog of rude manners and bad dress. Rumpled hat askew, sprawled in a chair, nonchalantly smoking a cigar, he seems no match for the dapper, poised, but decidedly supercilious, city gentleman sporting a ring on his little finger. Although the young lady gestures toward her country neighbor, spittoon at his feet like a faithful dog, her eyes are fastened with adoration on the city slicker.

In Tompkins Matteson's *Now or Never* of 1849, the young man waits for the reluctant young woman to decide between himself and the world of her parents (*Ill. 48*). She, however, inclines toward the open window—a common metaphor for freedom in 19th-century painting.[31] At a time when women had practically no legal or political rights, either as a daughter or as a wife, it is no wonder that she should hesitate.

Not surprisingly, paintings of women represent them in the home and often in the kitchen with the children. In Matteson's *Caught in the Act* of about 1860, the young woman has to cope with the naughty boy who has broken the jar (*Ill. 49*). In James Clonney's *Mother's Watch* of about 1852–56, the children play with the pocket watch while the mother sleeps (*Ill. 50*). Good food and happy children characterize Clonney's *The Good Breakfast* of 1852 (*Ill. 51*). The virtues of the home were propagated by *Godey's Ladies Book,* a monthly journal which reached the height of its popularity from about 1837, when Sarah J. Hale became its editor, until the mid-1850s, although the magazine continued for several more decades.[32] The journal included sentimental stories, prayers, plans of model cottages, fashion plates, household tips, and comments on culture. The engraved illustrations tended to dwell on home life—grandfathers and children occupying themselves with virtuous activities.

Accustomed to a life of domestic work, which was idealized by the ladies' magazines, a woman could hardly be expected to succeed as a professional painter. This, however, was accomplished by Lilly Martin Spencer, who managed to have thirteen children while producing a large *oeuvre* of genre paintings and portraits. The subjects she chose were domestic—women in the kitchen or with children. In *Shake Hands?* of 1854 and *Kiss Me and You'll Kiss the 'Lasses* of 1856, young women occupy themselves with making things to eat, creating the sustenance of life with their own hands (as Spencer was doing when she painted), and defying the viewer with frankly flirtatious smiles (*Ills. 52, 53*). Still-life arrangements had served as compositional foils in the works of Mount, Edmonds, and Matteson, but in Spencer's paintings the pans of fruit and baskets of vegetables reinforce the content of domestic abundance and vitality.

Women did get out to shop, as illustrated in *Interior of a Butcher Shop,* done in 1837 by an anonymous painter (*Ill. 54*). The top hats and genteel clothes of the two butchers emphasize the dignity of these artisans. On the other hand, solemnity marks

46. William Sidney Mount. *The Sportsman's Last Visit*, 1835. Oil on canvas, 21½ x 17½ inches. Suffolk Museum & Carriage House, Stony Brook, Long Island, New York. Melville Collection.

47. Francis William Edmonds. *The City and the Country Beaux* (1840). Oil on canvas, 20⅛ x 24¼ inches. Sterling and Francine Clark Art Institute, Williamstown, Massachusetts.

48. Tompkins Harrison Matteson. *Now or Never,* 1849. Oil on canvas, 27 x 34 inches. Parrish Art Museum, Southampton, New York.

49. Tompkins Harrison Matteson. *Caught in the Act,* c. 1860. Oil on canvas, 22 x 18 inches. Vassar College Art Gallery, Poughkeepsie, New York. Gift of Matthew Vassar, 1864.

50. James Goodwyn Clonney. *Mother's Watch*, c. 1852–56. Oil on canvas, 27 x 22 inches. Hirschl and Adler Galleries, New York.

51. James Goodwyn Clonney. *The Good Breakfast,* 1852. Oil on canvas, 17 x 14 inches. Collection of Jo Ann and Julian Ganz, Jr., Los Angeles.

53. Lilly Martin Spencer. *Shake Hands?*, 1854. Oil on canvas, 30⅛ x 25⅛ inches. Ohio Historical Center, Columbus.

52. Lilly Martin Spencer. *Kiss Me and You'll Kiss the 'Lasses,* 1856. Oil on canvas, 30⅛ x 25⅛ inches. The Brooklyn Museum. A. Augustus Healy Fund.

54. Unknown artist. *Interior of a Butcher Shop*, 1837. Oil on canvas, 26¾ x 30¾ inches. The Newark Museum, Newark, New Jersey. Gift of William F. Laporte, 1925.

the young women at an employment agency in William Henry Burr's *Intelligence Office* of 1840 (*Ill. 55*). Against the austere surroundings of the office, with only a clock and a sign declaring the honesty of the domestics, two working women stand in apprehension while the prospective employer, her élite social status declared by her gloves, parasol, and elaborate silken hat, ponders her choice. The New York newspaper *The Sun* lies on the bare floorboards; women seated on benches in the background exchange grim glances. The agent waits patiently for the lady's decision and his own commission.

Depictions of the conditions of working-class women seem to be rare early in the century. Although often disregarded as rewarding subjects for paintings after the Civil War, many illustrators, such as Solomon Eytinge, Charles Dana Gibson, and others, drew the female proletariat with compassion for *Harper's Weekly, Frank Leslie's Illustrated Weekly,* and other journals and newspapers.

46

55. William Henry Burr, *Intelligence Office,* 1840. Oil on canvas, 22 x 27 inches. The New-York Historical Society, New York.

Social Reality in Pre-Civil War Paintings

The decades of the 1840s, 1850s, and 1860s were a period of expansion as Americans moved west. Land in the western regions was surveyed, plotted, and sold to enterprising speculators. James Henry Beard, who became an itinerant painter in the frontier cities of Pittsburgh, Louisville, and in the South before settling permanently in Cincinnati, painted a number of paintings of western emigrants and frontier types. His *Ohio Land Speculator* of 1840 satirizes a confused neophyte in real estate transactions (*Ill. 56*).

George Caleb Bingham depicted the edge of the frontier in his paintings done in the late 1840s of raftsmen on the Missouri. River traffic was one of the most popular means of conveying cargo from the northern territories to the large cities. During the long journey, raftsmen occupied their time exchanging stories and playing cards. In *Raftsmen Playing Cards* of 1847, Bingham drew upon a subject traditional in the history of art, that of men playing cards, but placed the scene outdoors with specific details of American frontier life (*Ill. 57*).

The transient nature of American life was revealed in paintings of people on the move. Richard Caton Woodville's *The Card Players* of 1846 represents travelers with food baskets and trunks strewn about the waiting room while they idle away their time with a game of cards (*Ill. 58*). Francis William Edmonds's *Taking the Census* of 1854 refers to the burgeoning growth in population (*Ill. 59*). From 1840 to 1860 the census climbed from about 17 million to over 31 million, with the greatest growth occurring in the cities. In that time span, New York City jumped from 312,000 to 1,200,000; Chicago from 250 to 109,000.[33]

Immigration accounted for a large part of the increase; from 1840 to 1850 over one and a half million Europeans had moved to America, largely from Ireland and Germany. In the following decade, two and a half million came.[34] In deference to social reality, Charles F. Blauvelt's *The German Immigrant Inquiring His Way* of 1855 represents an old German soldier, perhaps a casualty of the wars of 1848, asking directions from a black woodchopper (*Ill. 60*).

Blauvelt's *Waiting for the Cars* of about 1858 depicts the interior of an inn, where a woman traveler

56. James Henry Beard. *The Ohio Land Speculator,* 1840. Oil on canvas, 19¾ x 24¼ inches. Hirschl and Adler Galleries, New York.

57. George Caleb Bingham. *Raftsmen Playing Cards* (1847). Oil on canvas, 28 x 36 inches. The St. Louis Art Museum. Ezra H. Linley Fund.

58. Richard Caton Woodville. *The Card Players,* 1846. Oil on canvas, 18½ x 25 inches. The Detroit Institute of Arts.

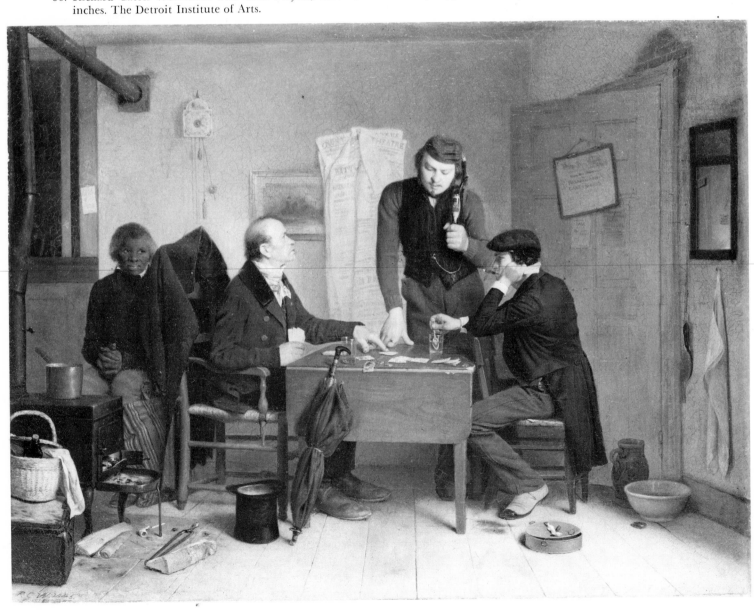

59. Francis William Edmonds. *Taking the Census,* 1854. Oil on canvas, 28 x 38 inches. Private collection, New York. Photograph courtesy of The Brooklyn Museum.

60. Charles F. Blauvelt. *The German Immigrant Inquiring His Way,* 1855. Oil on canvas, 36 x 29 inches. North Carolina Museum of Art, Raleigh.

61. Charles F. Blauvelt. *Waiting for the Cars,* c. 1858. Oil on canvas, 22 x 30 inches.
Private collection, New York.

nurses her baby and others warm themselves at the stove (*Ill. 61*). They are probably waiting for the train, for during the 1850s the railroad replaced the stagecoach as the most convenient and popular mode of travel between the major cities of the East.[35]

Later Edward Lamson Henry made a specialty of painting railroad trains. Some of his train pictures were historical recreations, portraits of famous railroad engines; others, such as *The Station on the Morris and Essex Railroad* of about 1864, attempted to capture the bustle and anticipation of passengers waiting at the station (*Ill. 62*).

The political situation in the country became more heated in the late 1840s as a result of the growing tensions with Mexico, which erupted into war in 1848, and the issue of slavery. Paintings done at the time reflect the new concerns. John Lewis Krimmel had copied David Wilkie's *Village Politicians* early in the century; local politicians figured in a number of other genre works, including James Clonney's *Politicians in a Country Bar* of 1844. However, the late 1840s saw a marked increase of paintings depicting local farmers reading newspapers and arguing political issues. Two men discuss politics in

Clonney's *Mexican News* of 1847 (*Ill. 63*). In Woodville's version of the subject *War News from Mexico* of about 1848, the central figure reads the "extra" edition of the newspaper which has just arrived at the post office (*Ill. 64*). Others crowd around him. The black man sits on the outside steps, apart from the proceedings, intently listening but not participating. In Woodville's *Politics in an Oyster House* of 1848, one man aggressively makes a point from his newspaper, while his elderly companion looks up at the spectator with an expression of patient boredom (*Ill. 65*). In all of these works newspapers are an important motif. Newspapers represent topicality; indeed, they were the means by which news of events reached the population in the countryside and on the frontier.

Related to politics was the courtroom. In Tompkins Matteson's *Justice's Court in the Backwoods* of 1850, the "justice" (who seems to earn his livelihood from cobbling) listens to the argument of one self-styled lawyer, while another bespectacled gentleman points to earlier precedent in the law book (*Ill. 66*).

An artist who exploited more fully the American voting system as a source for pictorial compositions was George Caleb Bingham. Bingham was himself involved in Whig politics in his native Missouri. In 1846 he lost in his effort to represent his district in the Missouri State Legislature, but two years later he won against the incumbent. In the meantime, he painted his first recorded political subject, *Stump Orator* (whereabouts unknown).[36]

Sometime early in 1851 Goupil & Co., the French publishing firm with offices in New York, commissioned Bingham to paint *Canvassing for a Vote* as a design for a lithograph (*Ill. 68*). The painting depicts an earnest young man leaning forward in his chair to make a point to three rural and somewhat skeptical types. In 1851 Bingham also began one of his most ambitious pictures, *The County Election* (*Ill. 67*). The extensive range of facial expressions suggests that he made use of handbooks on physiognomic expression.[37] However, the emphasis upon unattractive types indicates that the work may be a subtle indictment of the new laws which extended the franchise to the propertyless classes. Rather than the healthy, hearty "common man" of the American myth, we find this social comment replete with drunkards, bums, and avaricious schemers. Bingham had written on several occasions of his contempt for the radical politics of the "Locofocos."[38]

62. Edward Lamson Henry. *The Station on the Morris and Essex Railroad*, c. 1864. Oil on canvas, 11 x 20 inches. The Chase Manhattan Bank Art Collection, New York.

63. James Goodwyn Clonney. *Mexican News,* 1847. Oil on canvas, 26⅝ x 21¾ inches. Munson-Williams-Proctor Institute, Utica, New York.

64. Richard Caton Woodville. *War News from Mexico* (1848). Oil on canvas, 27 x 24¾ inches. The National Academy of Design, New York.

65. Richard Caton Woodville. *Politics in an Oyster House*, 1848. Oil on canvas, 16 x 13 inches. The Walters Art Gallery, Baltimore.

66. Tompkins Harrison Matteson. *Justice's Court in the Backwoods* (1850). Oil on canvas, 31¾ x 44 inches. New York State Historical Association, Cooperstown.

67. George Caleb Bingham. *The County Election*, 1851–52. Oil on canvas, 35⁷/₁₆ x 48¾ inches. The Boatmen's National Bank of St. Louis.

68. George Caleb Bingham. *Canvassing for a Vote,* 1852. Oil on canvas, 25⅛ x 30³⁄₁₆ inches. Nelson Gallery-Atkins Museum, Kansas City. Nelson Fund.

69. Arthur Fitzwilliam Tait. *Arguing the Point, Settling the Presidency,* 1854. Oil on wood, 19¾ x 24 inches. The R. W. Norton Art Gallery, Shreveport, La.

Black People in Pre-Civil War Painting

In the early 19th century, one or two blacks often appeared in paintings of the daily life of white people to denote the scene as specifically American. In these integrated scenes, blacks sit on stoops, lean against doorways, or find themselves teased by white boys.

Images of groups of blacks, removed from the company of white people, also occurred. The German-born Christian Mayr, who painted portraits in and around Charleston, South Carolina, in the 1840s, exhibited *Kitchen Ball at White Sulphur Springs* at the annual National Academy of Design exhibition in 1845. The title suggests that Mayr had witnessed a real event (*Ill. 70*). In the painting he has represented black people, well-groomed and dressed in party finery, enjoying the pleasures of a formal ball. No condescension colors the painting; however, Mayr's scene must have been rare in slaveholding America. When shown in New York, the effect must have been reassuring to the consciences of liberal Easterners who wanted to avoid the issue of human bondage.

European visitors who toured America in pre-Civil War days were unanimously shocked by slavery. Mrs. Frances Trollope, the sharp-tongued mother of Anthony Trollope, gathered her observations of American character in her *Domestic Manners of the Americans,* published in 1832. She strongly condemned the American attitude toward blacks and Indians.

. . . You will see them with one hand hoisting the cap of liberty, and with the other flogging their slaves. You will see them one hour lecturing their mob on the indefeasible [sic] rights of man, and the next driving from their homes the children of the soil, whom they have bound themselves to protect by the most solemn treaties.[39]

Charles Dickens visited America in 1842, and wrote of his experiences in *American Notes*. His criticism of slavery was incisive and harsh.

In 1849 there were fifteen free and fifteen slave states, giving the South equality in the Senate. However, the application of California for statehood as a free state precipitated a crisis. In 1850 the Whigs and Democrats in the Congress worked out the Compromise Bill which included a new Fugitive Slave Act. Under its severe terms, any black accused of being a runaway slave lost all rights; he could be remanded to slavery upon the presentation of an affidavit by any white man claiming ownership. Moreover, stiff penalties were levied against anyone aiding runaway slaves. The act fanned the antislavery fervor in the North. Harriet Beecher Stowe, daughter of the Reverend Lyman Beecher, responded to the injustice of the act by writing *Uncle Tom's Cabin,* which was serialized in the abolitionist newspaper *National Era* in 1851–52. Issued in book form

70. Christian Mayr. *Kitchen Ball at White Sulphur Springs,* 1838. Oil on canvas, 24 x 29½ inches. North Carolina Museum of Art, Raleigh.

in 1852, it sold more than 300,000 copies in the first year.[40]

In her moving account of the fortunes of a family of slaves wrenched apart by the caprices of their owners and the fluctuations of the market, Stowe created vivid portraits: Simon Legree as the personification of evil; Topsy, the scatterbrained child; the saintly Little Eva, and Tom himself—the black "noble savage" of the abolitionists. But Stowe also perpetuated racial stereotypes. Of blacks she generalized, "They are not naturally daring and enterprising, but home-loving and affectionate."[41a]

In spite of many shortcomings, Stowe's book was a strong indictment of the inhumanity of the slave system. She devoted several pages to describing the slave market of New Orleans:

A slave warehouse! Perhaps some of my readers conjure up horrible visions of such a place. They fancy some foul, obscure den . . . . But no, innocent friend; in these days men have learned the art of sinning expertly and genteelly, so as not to shock the eyes and senses of respectable society. Human property is high in the market; and is, therefore, well fed, well cleaned, tended, and looked after, that it may come to sale sleek, and strong, and shining. A slave warehouse in New Orleans is a house externally not much unlike many others, kept with neatness . . . .

Then you shall be courteously entreated to call and examine, and shall find an abundance of husbands, wives, brothers, sisters, fathers, mothers, and young children, to be "sold separately, or in lots, to suit the convenience of the

71. Eyre Crowe. *Slave Market in Richmond, Virginia* (1852). Oil on canvas, 21¾ x 32 inches. Collection of the Honorable and Mrs. H. John Heinz III, Washington, D.C. Photograph courtesy Kennedy Galleries, Inc., New York.

purchaser;" and that soul immortal, once bought with blood and anguish by the Son of God, when the earth shook, and the rocks were rent, and the graves were opened, can be sold, leased, mortgaged, exchanged for groceries or dry goods, to suit the phases of trade, or the fancy of the purchaser.[41b]

Stowe's account apparently inspired a number of slave-market scenes in the 1850s. One of the most poignant was *Slave Market in Richmond, Virginia,* painted in 1852 by Eyre Crowe when he accompanied William Makepeace Thackeray on his lecture tour of America (*Ill. 71*). Crowe described the circumstances in his *With Thackeray in America,* published in 1893.

On rough benches were sitting, huddled close together, neatly dressed in grey, young negro girls with white collars fastened by scarlet bows, and in white aprons. The form of a woman clasping her infant, ever touching, seemed the more so here. There was a muscular field-labourer sitting apart; a rusty old stove filled up another space. Having rapidly sketched these features, I had not time to put my outline away before the whole group of buyers and dealers were in the compartment. I thought the best plan was to go on unconcernedly; but, perceiving me so engaged, no one would bid. The auctioneer, who had mounted his table, came down and asked me whether, "if I had a business store, and someone came in and interrupted my trading, I should like it." This was unanswerable; I got up with the intention of leaving quietly, but, feeling this would savour of flight, I turned around to the now evidently angry crowd of dealers, and said, "You may turn me away, but I can recollect all I have seen."[42]

Crowe left the auction rooms. Thackeray apparently was not pleased with the actions of his amanuensis. Crowe continued the account:

"Crowe has been very imprudent," Thackeray wrote to a friend afterwards. And, in truth, I soon reflected it was so. It might have led to unpleasant results to the lecturer himself, bound, as he went South, not to be embroiled in any untoward accident involving interference with the question of slavery, then at fever-heat, owing to Mrs. Stowe's fiery denunciations in "Uncle Tom's Cabin."[43]

In general, artists found that representations of slave markets were bad business; John Rogers, the sculptor of small genre sculptures, offered casts of his *Slave Auction* for sale in 1859, only a few weeks after the execution of John Brown (*Ill. 72*). The work, however, did not sell as he had expected, and by Christmas Eve he confessed: "I find the times have quite headed me off . . . for the Slave Auction tells such a strong story that none of the stores will receive it to sell for fear of offending their Southern customers."[44]

72. John Rogers. *Slave Auction,* 1859. Plaster. The New-York Historical Society, New York.

Not offensive to public taste—whether pro- or anti-abolitionist—was Eastman Johnson's *Negro Life in the South,* later popularly known as *Old Kentucky Home,* which was exhibited at the National Academy of Design's spring exhibition of 1859 and which catapulted Johnson to fame (*Ill. 73*). In this work Johnson portrays blacks in a variety of activities which we have come to recognize as racial stereotypes: playing banjoes, shuffling to music, courting idly, and fondling children. Compared with Eyre Crowe's painting, Johnson's work is a fancifully staged concoction.

During the 1860s painters in the North, including Johnson, turned to black subjects with increasing frequency. Later, Henry T. Tuckerman was to say of Johnson's paintings of blacks:

In his delineation of the negro, Eastman Johnson has achieved a peculiar fame. One may find in his best pictures of this class a better insight into the normal character of that unfortunate race than ethnological discussion often yields. The affection, the humor, the patience and serenity which redeem from brutality and ferocity the civilized though subjugated African, are made to appear in the creations of this artist with singular authenticity. . . . "The Old Kentucky Home" is not only a masterly work of art, full of nature, truth, local significance, and character, but it illustrates a phase of American life which the rebellion and its consequences will either uproot or essentially modify; and therefore this picture is as valuable as a memorial as it is interesting as an art-study.[45]

A memorial, indeed, was painted by John Antrobus, a little-known artist. The figures in his *Plantation Burial* are gathered in the forest in mourning as they bury a fellow slave (*Ill. 74*).

73. Eastman Johnson. *Negro Life in the South (Old Kentucky Home),* 1859. Oil on canvas, 36 x 45 inches. The New-York Historical Society, New York.

74. John Antrobus. *Plantation Burial,* c. 1860. Oil on canvas, 53 x 81½ inches. The Historic New Orleans Collection.

Response to the Civil War

The event most disruptive to the lives of Americans —black and white—was the war between the states. The optimistic belief in the possibilities of equality and visions of the attainment of the simple, agrarian life, which existed among many intellectuals and writers before the 1860s, was shattered by the reality that thirteen Southern states would rather go to war than extend the concept of equality to the black races and give up an economic system that depended upon slavery.

When Charles C. Ingham, acting for the President of the National Academy of Design, delivered the Academy's annual report on May 8, 1861, he spoke for a number of artists in the first flush of patriotic enthusiasm:

The great Rebellion has startled society from its propriety, and war and politics now occupy every mind. No one thinks of the *Arts.* Even among the Artists, patriotism has superseded painting, and many have laid by the palette and pencil to shoulder the musket.[46]

Some artists, for example the landscape painters Sanford Gifford and Jervis McEntee, enlisted in the Union Army as a matter of conscience. Others, in search of topical subjects for the weekly journals, obtained permission to follow the troops.

Winslow Homer, only twenty-five years old when the war began, joined the Union campaigns as an artist-reporter for *Harper's Weekly,* which engraved and published his quick, summary sketches. L. Prang & Company, which had published maps of the battle-

75. Winslow Homer. *Home, Sweet Home,* c. 1863. Oil on canvas, 21 x 15¾ inches. Collection of Mrs. Nathan Shaye, Detroit.

76. Winslow Homer. *The Last Goose at Yorktown,* c. 1863. Oil on canvas, 14¼ x 18¼ inches. Kennedy Galleries, Inc., New York.

fields and portraits of Civil War generals, commissioned Homer to design a set of Campaign Sketches in 1863. These "sketches" portray humorous incidents around the camps.[47]

In 1863 Homer turned some of his working drawings into oil paintings and sent *Home, Sweet Home* and *The Last Goose at Yorktown* to the annual spring exhibition of the National Academy of Design (*Ills. 75, 76*). The title of *Home, Sweet Home* refers to the popular song, the strains of which were heard in many bivouacked camps. Both the standing soldier and the seated one, with pen in hand writing a letter, pause and reflect. The war was long and Homer has captured what was to him the essence of war—waiting and boredom.

Moreover, the Army diet was notoriously poor and soldiers had to use their own initiative to supplement their fare with more appetizing food. Raids upon the local civilization population were common. In Homer's frankly anecdotal *The Last Goose at Yorktown,* two soldiers creep up on an apparently unsuspecting goose. Edwin Forbes was another Civil War artist who chronicled the more unheroic moments of the troops. His young man in *Drummer Boy Cooling His Coffee,* seated on his own drum before his camouflaged tent, grimaces as he blows on his steaming, boiled coffee (*Ill. 77*).

To the acerbic vision of David Gilmour Blythe, the war was a political and social horror. His didactic but emotionally charged *Libby Prison* of 1863 (Museum of Fine Arts, Boston)* sketches the squalid depths of the infamous Confederate prison. His *Post Office* of about 1862–64 sharply renders the shoving crowds pressing to receive the latest mail (*Ill. 78*). Even at the height of the war, it is "business as usual" for the young pickpocket filching the wallet of a preoccupied, silk-hatted gentleman.

The majority of paintings exhibited at the time of the Civil War were sentimental renditions of life at home—of the home folks thinking of their loved ones and children playing soldiers and nurses. The gal-

* The specific paintings discussed in the text but not illustrated are followed by the names of their owners enclosed in parentheses.

lery-visiting public identified more with familiar scenes. In Homer's *The Initials,* exhibited in the spring of 1865, the young woman leans against the tree which bears the carved initials and insignias of her beloved, as well as his memory (*Ill. 80*).

A great number of Civil War subjects were painted right after the war when the danger was over but sentiment still ran high. Lilly Martin Spencer's *The War Spirit at Home—Celebrating the Victory at Vicksburg* of 1866 presents children gaily marching about the dining room while their mother and the servant soberly reflect on the news of the day (*Ill. 79*). The mother precariously balances her youngest in her lap while reading the *New York Times.* Her status as head of the household (while her husband is absent) is declared by the fact that *she* holds the newspaper, that 19th-century symbol of authority.

Another painter of sentimental war subjects was George Cochran Lambdin. His *Consecration, 1861* (*Ill. 81*) was praised by Henry T. Tuckerman: "His picture called the 'Consecration, 1861,' represents a

77. Edwin Forbes. *Drummer Boy Cooling His Coffee,* c. 1860–64. Oil on canvas, 12 x 10 inches. Amherst College Collection, Amherst, Massachusetts.

78. David Gilmour Blythe. *Post Office,* c. 1862–64. Oil on canvas, 24 x 20 inches. Museum of Art, Carnegie Institute, Pittsburgh.

79. Lilly Martin Spencer. *The War Spirit at Home—Celebrating the Victory at Vicksburg,* 1866. Oil on canvas, 30 x 32¾ inches. The Newark Museum, Newark, New Jersey.

80. Winslow Homer. *The Initials*, 1864. Oil on canvas, 15½ x 11½ inches.
Collection of Dr. and Mrs. Irving Levitt, New York.

young volunteer officer parting from his sweetheart, who kisses his sword, and thereby dedicates it to freedom and victory."[48] The same officer appears again in Lambdin's *Winter Quarters in Virginia,* sitting alone in his tent, wrapped in his thoughts of love and war *(Ill. 82).* There is anecdote in Lambdin's paintings but few expressive gestures; mood substitutes for action.

Winslow Homer's *Prisoners from the Front,* exhibited in 1866, established Homer's reputation *(Ill. 83).* On the barren battlefield and accompanied by their guard, the Confederate soldiers—a worried boy, a humbled but wary old man, and a yet defiant young man— have laid down their rifles and confront the young Union officer who will decide their fate. The Union officer, his hands behind him, seems to be in no hurry. The confrontation has no moralizing or melodramatic overtones—no heroes or villains—simply men whom the outcome of the war has decreed will be winners and losers. The painting confronts the spectator with the same reportorial objectivity as a war photograph by Timothy O'Sullivan[49] *(Ill. 84).*

The most poignant theme to come from the war

81. George Cochran Lambdin. *The Consecration, 1861,* 1865. Oil on canvas, 24 x 18¼ inches. Indianapolis Museum of Art. James E. Roberts Fund.

was that of slaves escaping to liberty. Contemporary stories of the bravery of black slaves escaping on the Underground Railroad must have inspired a number of artists. In the early 1860s Eastman Johnson painted several versions of *A Ride for Liberty—The Fugitive Slaves,* depicting a family of four astride a galloping horse, an incident which Johnson claimed to have seen on the morning of March 23, 1862, as General George McClellan's forces were advancing on Manassas[50] (*Ill. 85*). Theodor Kaufmann painted *On to Liberty* in 1867, showing a number of slave women and children hurrying out of the woods (*Ill. 86*).

Worry and concern mark the faces of the adults and older children who carry and drag the smaller ones in their haste to make the safety of a Union encampment.

In contrast to the painting by Kaufmann, Thomas Moran's *Slaves Escaping Through the Swamp* of 1863 emphasizes the hostile environment surrounding the escaping slaves (*Ill. 87*). Wading through the swamp in their attempt to throw off the pursuing bloodhounds, the entanglements of the swamp appear dense and unrelieved.

Right after the war the transient black man be-

82. George Cochran Lambdin. *Winter Quarters in Virginia—Army of the Potomac, 1864,* 1866. Oil on canvas, 16 x 20 inches. Private collection. Photograph courtesy of Berry-Hill Galleries, New York.

83. Winslow Homer. *Prisoners from the Front*, 1866. Oil on canvas, 24 x 38 inches. The Metropolitan Museum of Art, New York. Gift of Mrs. Frank B. Porter, 1922.

84. Timothy O'Sullivan. *Confederate Prisoners*, 1863. Photograph, 4 x 5 inches. Library of Congress, Washington, D.C.

85. Eastman Johnson. *A Ride for Liberty
   —The Fugitive Slaves* (1863). Oil on
   canvas, 21¾ x 26¼ inches. The Brooklyn Museum. Gift of Miss Gwendolyn
   O. L. Conkling.

86. Theodor Kaufmann. *On to Liberty,*
   1867. Oil on canvas, 36 x 56 inches.
   Hirschl and Adler Galleries, New
   York.

came a reality as families of blacks left the barren soil of the South for the Northern cities. The itinerant black fiddler in Johnson's *Fiddling His Way* is dignified, serious, and manly (*Ill. 88*). The painting traveled to Paris where it hung in the United States section of the 1867 Universal Exposition to advertise the new, "emancipated" status of black people.

In 1872 James Beard painted *Goodbye, Ole Virginia,* representing a family of blacks on the road with the family dog, a cow, and a few belongings (*Ill. 89*). Waving farewell to the old homestead, the parents look back; the two children, however, look forward into the future.

In the late 1870s Winslow Homer traveled to the South where he painted a number of blacks working in the cotton fields. Thomas Pollock Anshutz and Thomas Eakins also painted realistic scenes of blacks in the 1880s; later Thomas Hovenden and Henry O. Tanner painted blacks with sympathy and a measure of sentimentality.

In general, blacks were no longer included in scenes of white American life. Before the war, the subordinate status of blacks had the backing of law —pictorially, they had their place on the stoop or outside the door. After the war had been won and the slaves freed from their legal bondage, the North turned its attention to other matters and left the job of "reconstruction" to former slaveowners and "carpetbaggers" more unscrupulous than previous slave jobbers. The economic lot of the ex-slave hardly improved while the North focused on the work of conquering the Western plains, building up a united nation, and joining the world powers. In terms of images, white painters had difficulties incorporating the "freed" blacks into integrated scenes of "respectable" gentility, except where they functioned as servants. The artists did not escape the hypocrisy and prejudices of their time. Faced with a society in which blacks were mistreated, it is not surprising that in the paintings of middle-class, urban life, which appeared in the 1870s and 1880s, blacks virtually disappeared.

87. Thomas Moran. *Slaves Escaping Through the Swamp,* 1863. Oil on canvas, 34 x 44 inches. Philbrook Art Center, Tulsa, Oklahoma. Gift of Laura A. Clubb, 1947.

88. Eastman Johnson. *Fiddling His Way,* 1866. Oil on canvas, 23¾ x 35½ inches. Coe Kerr Gallery, Inc., and M. Knoedler & Co., Inc., New York.

89. James Henry Beard. *Goodbye, Ole Virginia,* 1872. Oil on canvas, 25 x 35½ inches. Photograph courtesy of J. N. Bartfield Galleries, New York.

Post-Civil War Years: Urbanization

America emerged at the conclusion of four years of war a different nation. From a low point in 1865 when Abraham Lincoln was assassinated, the nation moved into a period of rapid growth. Expansion in population, in territory, and in economic wealth characterized the country in the late 1860s. Technological progress brought profound changes that affected all Americans, as well as, ultimately, the rest of the world. The Atlantic cable was laid in 1866, the Central Pacific and Union Pacific railways were united at Promontory Point in Utah in 1869, and the Suez Canal was completed in 1869. Mark Twain and Charles Dudley Warner defined the time in *The Gilded Age: A Tale of Today* (1873):

> The eight years in America from 1860 to 1868 uprooted institutions that were centuries old, changed the politics of a people, transformed the social life of half the country, and wrought so profoundly upon the entire national character that the influence cannot be measured short of two or three generations.[51]

The old country ways, whatever their charm, could no longer cope with the complexities of urbanization. The small-peddler methods of retailing were obsolete. America progressed from mercantilism toward international capitalism, and newly prosperous financiers and industrialists moved from modest townhouses to palatial mansions brimming over with European art.

The transitions were not always smooth and the hold of tradition exerted its influence. Although the younger and more "advanced" artists turned to the American city and middle-class leisure life as sources of subjects for their paintings, many painters continued to rely on the themes left over from pre-Civil War days. Pictures of children, American farm life, old people, and historical genre appealed to those who were more comfortable with familiar, nostalgic, and patriotic scenes.

The most sentimental pictures of the time were of children. Children had been painted throughout the 1840s and 1850s; the records of the exhibitions at the National Academy of Design and the American Art-Union attest to the great number of idealized representations of children. In the 1850s influential journals such as *The Crayon* and the *Cosmopolitan Art Journal* praised paintings of children, and the poets of the time eulogized the innocence of childhood. The Civil War did not discourage the output. Indeed, the child seemed to be glorified more than ever. Henry T. Tuckerman, critic of and for his age, viewed the child as the redeeming solace of art and life. Devoting a whole article to children for *The Galaxy* in 1867, his effusive remarks were typical of the times:

> Always and everywhere the image of childhood to poet and painter, to the landscape, the household, the shrine, the temple and the grave . . . is a redeeming presence, a harmonizing and hopeful element, the token of what we were, and prophecy of what we may be.[52]

To Tuckerman, the image of the child returned man to innocence and nature:

> We become little children in art, in sentiment, in method and spirit whenever and wherever we seize a type of the beautiful, an emanation of the divine, a principle of the true. Wherein consists the grace of the most effective school of modern art, pictorial and musical, but in this return to nature?[53]

At the end of the 1860s another well-known art critic, Eugene Benson, wrote "Childhood in Modern Literature" for *Appleton's Journal*. In Victorian America Benson's saccharine outpourings were not extraordinary:

> The child—the sanctity, freshness, and mystery of child-life—in literature, owes its advancement beyond the idea of a healthy little animal to the worship of the infant Jesus. In contemporary literature childhood is a special and individual presence, not an accidental and accessory one. . . .

... Hail to the children! Their glad faces, their fleeting tears, their playfulness, have interested us more than "Tom Jones" or the "Red-Cross Knight." . . . Children! They rule the world.[54]

For a popular audience Currier & Ives published numerous prints of children, as did Louis Prang, who developed a process for making inexpensive colored lithographs. Among the many "chromolithographs" of idealized children issued was Eastman Johnson's design for *The Barefoot Boy,* inspired by the lines from Whittier:

> Blessings on thee, little man,
> Barefoot boy, with cheek of tan.[55]

Many paintings of children locate them on the farm engaged in adult tasks, as does Charles Caleb Ward's *Force and Skill (Ill. 90).* Recalling earlier subjects of scythe-grinding by Edmonds, Mount, and Johnson, the farmyard scene depicts one child turn-ing the grindstone while the other boy sharpens the knife. The moral exists in the title: Physical strength and mental skill must be equally applied to accomplish the tasks at hand. The painter idealized the farm as the place where unity and cooperation could exist.

Another painter of adolescent children was Seymour Joseph Guy. His *Making a Train* of 1867 represents a young girl stepping out of her dress in such a way as to create a train of drapery falling behind her *(Ill. 91).* She is playing at being a woman; with her chemise slipping over her shoulders, the pubescent, erotic content is none too subtle.

Scenes of children playing outdoors were equally popular. Moreover, outdoor scenes gave artists the opportunity to paint in the newer styles, emphasizing a lighter palette. Eastman Johnson's *Old Stage Coach* of 1871 (Milwaukee Art Center) portrayed the preciousness of childhood make-believe; the coach itself was an explicitly nostalgic stage setting. Homer's *Snap the Whip* of 1872 displayed the energy and

90. Charles Caleb Ward. *Force and Skill,* 1869. Oil on canvas, 12 x 10 inches. Currier Gallery of Art, Manchester, New Hampshire.

75

91. Seymour Joseph Guy. *Making a Train*, 1867. Oil on canvas, 18⅛ x 24⅜ inches. Philadelphia Museum of Art. George W. Elkins Collection.

92. Winslow Homer. *Snap the Whip*, 1872. Oil on canvas, 22¼ x 36½ inches. The Butler Institute of American Art, Youngstown, Ohio.

93. John George Brown. *Gathering Autumn Leaves*, 1875. Oil on canvas, 30⅛ x 25 inches. Private collection, New York.

94. William Hahn. *Learning the Lesson (Children Playing School)*, 1881. Oil on canvas, 34 x 27 inches. The Oakland Museum, Oakland, California. Gift of the Kahn Foundation.

rambunctiousness of childhood (*Ill. 92*). In the background of the Homer painting is a one-room schoolhouse.

Schooling became important to Americans; to the students of *McGuffey's Reader* education was a moral virtue. Many artists explored the theme of children learning. A young mother teaches her children about nature in John George Brown's *Gathering Autumn Leaves* of 1875, and William Hahn's *Learning the Lesson* of 1881 presents an older sister coaching her younger siblings in a drill (*Ills. 93, 94*).

Throughout the late 1860s and 1870s John Ehninger, Eastman Johnson, and Winslow Homer continued to paint scenes of children and also of farm life. These artists were lauded for rejecting subjects of contemporary life. George Sheldon praised Homer's outdoor paintings in his 1879 *American Painters:* "In the best of them may always be recognized a certain noble simplicity, quietude, and sobriety, that one feels grateful for in an age of gilded spread-eagleism. . . ."[56] Some of Homer's works, such as his *Song of the Lark*, with a tall farmer looking out over the horizon (*Ill. 95*), are close in feeling to those of the French painter Jean-François Millet. Critics extolled Johnson, whose *Corn Husking Bee* of 1876 was painted on Nantucket, the artist's summer home, calling him "a chronicler of a phase of our national life which is fast passing away"[57] (*Ill. 97*).

95. Winslow Homer. *Song of the Lark*, 1876. Oil on canvas, 38½ x 24 inches (sight). Private collection, New York. Photograph courtesy of Acquavella Galleries, New York.

96. John Whetten Ehninger. *October,* 1867. Oil on canvas, 32 x 54 inches.
   National Collection of Fine Arts, Smithsonian Institution, Washington, D.C.

97. Eastman Johnson. *Corn Husking Bee,* 1876. Oil on canvas, 27¼ x 54¼ inches.
   The Art Institute of Chicago. Potter Palmer Collection.

98. Thomas Waterman Wood. *The Yankee Peddler,* 1872. Oil on canvas, 28 x 40 inches. Collection of Mrs. Norman B. Woolworth, New York.

In turning to rural themes, such artists were reflecting the cultural protest against the Industrial Revolution. Many European artists had deplored the conditions of 19th-century capitalism: urban overcrowding, slum conditions, pollution, and human exploitation. Jean-François Millet venerated the poor and anonymous peasants as the last surviving species from a time when human labor had nobility and dignity. Most American painters, however, did not simply react against urban realities—they ignored them. To the makers and painters of the American myth, the hardships of poverty did not exist. In their world all Americans were good-natured, hardworking middle-class Yankees.

The painters of nostalgia also turned to old men and old women for subjects for their art. Thomas Waterman Wood's *The Yankee Peddler* of 1872 is not the virile man of Ehninger's 1853 version, but an old, white-haired, bearded man whose peddling ways were simply "quaint" (*Ill. 98*). Thomas Hicks in 1877 expressed the virtues of piety and fidelity, along with old age, in his *There's No Place Like Home,* depicting an elderly couple alone by the fire (*Ill. 99*). Another artist who mined the vein for nostalgia was Thomas Hovenden. His old people are unanimously virtuous and contented with their lot. His *Sunday Morning* of 1881 depicts an aging black couple pausing in their tasks in their picturesquely ramshackle abode (*Ill. 100*).

Platt Powell Ryder's *Patience* of 1884 is similar in mood to Eastman Johnson's *Embers (Ills. 101, 102).* In both paintings old men sit by the fire, leaning on an umbrella or a cane—dwelling on the days gone past. Toward the end of the century Henry O. Tanner painted *The Banjo Lesson,* representing an elderly black man teaching a young boy to play the musical instrument (*Ill. 103*). Tanner's paintings of blacks reflect his own black experience and religious upbringing, and a reverential mood predominates in almost all of his paintings.

99. Thomas Hicks. *There's No Place Like Home,* 1877. Oil on canvas, 21½ x 28½ inches. Schweitzer Gallery, New York.

100. Thomas Hovenden. *Sunday Morning,* 1881. Oil on canvas, 18¼ x 15½ inches. The Fine Arts Museums of San Francisco. Mildred Anna Williams Collection.

101. Platt Powell Ryder. *Patience,* 1884. Oil on canvas, 27⅛ x 22⅛ inches. Yale University Art Gallery, New Haven. John Hill Morgan Fund and Walter N. Frank, Jr. Fund.

102. Eastman Johnson. *Embers,* c. 1880. Oil on canvas, 13⅞ x 12⅝ inches. Private collection.

82

103.   Henry O. Tanner. *The Banjo Lesson,* 1893. Oil on canvas, 48½ x 35 inches.
Hampton Institute College Museum, Hampton, Virginia.

The Cosmopolitan Life

After the Civil War the majority of artists, and particularly the younger painters, turned to the urban environment for pictorial themes. The subjects that emerged as most popular to the painters of modern life involved art and music, leisure-time and vacation activities, and urban sports.

Depictions of outdoor city scenes peopled with middle-class promenaders and shoppers began long before the Civil War. There was, in fact, an even development from Krimmel's *View of Centre Square, on the 4th of July* (*Ill. 2*) to Hyppolite Sebron's *Broadway and Spring Street* of 1855 (*Ill. 104*). Sebron displays a bustling city with a variety of activities: Chinese men in their ethnic dress parade with placards advertising Barnum's circus, lady shoppers stroll in front of the Düsseldorf Gallery, and firemen race to a fire. Johannes Adam Simon Oertel's *Woodruff Stables, Jerome Avenue, The Bronx* of 1861 represents a group of gentlemen with tall, silken hats selecting from among the carriages (*Ill. 105*). Commissioned for lithographic publication and therefore intended for a large public, the Sebron and Oertel paintings seek to capture the panoramic heterogeneity of the city. But during the three decades after the Civil War, paintings of urban life tended to lose their topographical overtones to become private, intimate glimpses into the doings of the leisure classes.

Oertel's *Visiting Grandma* of 1865, painted the year the war ended, contains references to both the old and the new (*Ill. 106*). Grandma herself is well along in years, but she surrounds herself with her youthful grandchildren and objects of modern affluence. Symbolizing eclectic taste and modern convenience is the technologically up-to-date gas lamp on the center table, fashioned from a reproduction of Giovanni da Bologna's *Mercury*. A rubber hose extending from the chandelier above feeds gas into the lamp. The John Rogers sculpture *The Town Pump* and the fringed and overstuffed furniture were all part of recommended, contemporary interior decor.[58]

Artists again painted musicians—not the country fiddlers of Mount, but rather sober, serious musicians as in Homer's *Amateur Musicians* of 1867, where the cellist and violinist have propped their music sheets against their easels (*Ill. 107*). Their music is not for the local farmers but for themselves, and each is isolated in his own concentration.

John George Brown's *The Music Lesson* of 1870 focuses on middle-class involvement with cultural self-improvement (*Ill. 108*). Here, though, music is the occasion for a flirtation, and Brown dwells on the sociability of two people rather than their self-involvement in making art. In terms of the development of "genre" painting, Brown's work, with its emphasis on anecdote, is more old-fashioned than Homer's.

From our perspective, the 1870s was the decade in which the shift away from the old attitudes and old styles seems most noticeable. A myriad of factors produced the change—but the younger painters did pictures that had a newer look. In the older genre paintings, for example Edmonds's *The Country and the City Beaux* (*Ill. 47*), artists often painted figures of a different social class from their patrons. The scene could be looked into, as into a small shadow box, unrelated to the viewer's own space. The anecdotal, story-telling elements are marked—in his own imagination the viewer can construct the before and the after of the scene. He knows what the grimacing and gesticulating figures are thinking and the titles help in that identification. Moreover, social interaction and communal activities describe the content of the older genre painting.

But Thomas Eakins and other younger artists had different concerns; their approach to painting matched that of a growing number of European realists. When Eakins returned from Europe his earliest paintings involved one or two figures sitting at the Eakins's family piano, preoccupied with their music or resting from their playing. No story or narration concerns Eakins's *At the Piano* of 1870–71 (University Art Museum, University of Texas) and his *Home Scene* of 1870–71 (Brooklyn Museum). He evokes only a mood and atmosphere.

For *The Pathetic Song*, an ambitious painting of 1881, Eakins again chose his own friends and presented them in their own milieu (*Ill. 109*). Working with traditional old-master methods of underpainting and glazes, he painted specific people in a familiar,

and specific, scene. There is no touch of condescension toward his musicians, nor is there a story in the traditional sense. The space of *The Pathetic Song*, with its angled viewpoint, seems to be continuous with the viewer's; heightening the sense of reality, Eakins drew his signature in perspective as it would be seen on an actual floor. The description of light is more unified and natural than in the traditional genre scene by Mount or Edmonds. The singer, Miss Margaret Alexina Harrison, faces away from the left lateral light. The light catches in the folds of her pale lavender satin dress, accentuating the rich play of silver-colored reflections. Furthermore, Eakins chooses to have the figure of the singer appear in absolute and clear focus; the forms encircling the perimeter of this point of focus become increasingly blurred. The figures of Stoltz, the cellist, and Susan McDowell, the pianist (and later Eakins's wife), are submerged in shadow, each individualized and isolated although united in their music making.

The musical chamber group moved back into the artist's studio in Stacey Tolman's *The Musicale* of 1887 (*Ill. 110*). Similar to the Eakins, there is no story or anecdote. The viewer knows only that the trio plays Haydn from the title of the musical score resting on the music stand. Following the conventions of traditional genre, which included still-life elements, the artist has given careful attention to the art objects and paraphernalia of the studio—the Japanese umbrella, fur rug, studio props, porcelain vases, and other paintings that adorn the wall. Oriental vases decorate the settings of both Eakins's and Tolman's musicales.

The decade of the 1860s witnessed a renewed interest among Americans and Europeans in the Far East. Early in the 1850s Commodore Matthew Galbraith Perry had visited Japan. The report of his journey, published in 1856, contained facsimiles of three Japanese prints, and by 1860 Hokusai prints were circulating in Boston and New York. The artist John La Farge was an enthusiastic collector; in the mid-1860s he owned prints by many famous 18th- and 19th-century Japanese printmakers.[59]

In 1860 the Japanese Embassy arrived in New York. The officers of the National Academy of Design delayed the closing of the Annual Exhibition in June of that year in order to invite the Japanese dignitaries to a special viewing of the American paintings. The assumption that the Japanese would be interested in attending the viewing suggests a reciprocal interest in Japanese art on the part of the officers of the National Academy.[60] There are countless examples of incidents confirming that the vogue for things Japanese was strong among a select audience of art patrons. It comes as no surprise, then, that contemporary painting—portraits and interior scenes—began to include Eastern artworks as accessory motifs.

More relevant for the direction of the history of art was the adaptation by the more daring artists of the compositional devices of the Japanese print. James A. McNeill Whistler's *Lady of the Lange Lijsen* of 1864 depicts a woman in Oriental costume painting a porcelain vase (*Ill. 111*). The asymmetrical arrangement of the composition, the flat treatment of the forms, and the compressed space recalls the artistic conventions of Japanese prints. By 1867 the critic Russell Sturgis could describe an American work and praise its "flatness." Commenting on a contemporary work by the little-known painter William John Hennessy, Sturgis indicates his awareness of the Japanese print style:

> The persevering way in which Mr. Hennessy keeps his studies 'flat,' . . . aiming to achieve local truth of light and shade before he tries for 'effects,' is significant of good. If he is trying to gain through an almost Japanese flatness a more than Japanese brilliancy of color, and to add this to delicate and forcible drawing, he is trying for what is good.[61]

Whistler's painting, with its formal, decorative qualities, is an early statement of a trend toward aestheticism which reached a high point decades later.

Oriental artifacts accounted for only a fraction of the many objects with which successful artists filled their studios. The contents of William Merritt Chase's *In the Studio* exemplified the *horror vacui* and eclecticism of the times (*Ill. 112*). Not far in spirit from Oertel's *Visiting Grandma*, Chase's *In the*

104. Hyppolite Sebron. *Broadway and Spring Street*, 1855. Oil on canvas, 29¼ x 42½ inches. Graham Gallery and Schweitzer Gallery, New York.

105. Johannes Adam Simon Oertel. *Woodruff Stables, Jerome Avenue, The Bronx*, 1861. Oil on canvas, 24 x 39⅞ inches. Museum of the City of New York.

106. Johannes Adam Simon Oertel. *Visiting Grandma,* 1865. Oil on canvas, 24 x 20 inches. The New-York Historical Society, New York.

107. Winslow Homer. *Amateur Musicians*, 1867. Oil on canvas, 18 x 15 inches. The Metropolitan Museum of Art, New York. Samuel D. Lee Fund, 1939.

108. John George Brown. *The Music Lesson*, 1870. Oil on canvas, 24 x 20 inches. The Metropolitan Museum of Art, New York. Gift of Colonel Charles A. Fowler, 1921.

89

109. Thomas Eakins. *The Pathetic Song*, 1881. Oil on canvas, 45 x 32½ inches.
Corcoran Gallery of Art, Washington, D.C.

110. Stacey Tolman. *The Musicale,* 1887. Oil on canvas, 36⅛ x 46 inches. The Brooklyn Museum. Dick S. Ramsay Fund.

111. James A. McNeill Whistler. *Lady of the Lange Lijsen,* 1864. Oil on canvas, 36¼ x 24¼ inches. Courtesy of the John G. Johnson Collection, Philadelphia.

112. William Merritt Chase. *In the Studio,* c. 1880. Oil on canvas, 28½ x 40⅛ inches. The Brooklyn Museum. Gift of Mrs. C. H. De Silver, in memory of her husband.

113. Frank Waller. *Interior View of the Metropolitan Museum of Art when in Fourteenth Street,* 1881. Oil on canvas, 24 x 20 1/16 inches. The Metropolitan Museum of Art, New York. Purchase, 1895.

Studio exhibits an array of the artist's personal possessions: Renaissance chests, potted palms, deluxe illustrated books, model ships, musical instruments, Oriental fabrics, Japanese fans, framed European art, and French carpets. The materiality of objects of pecuniary worth and their variety of optical surfaces modified the impressionism of Chase. The objects were always too precious to be shattered by the homogeneous brush stroke. The woman with her book participates with the display—an object of beauty much like the deluxe book which commands her attention. Chase was only one of many artists with a broad range of sophisticated and cosmopolitan tastes.

The impulse to acquire and display works of art found its outlet in the movement to create grand municipal palaces of art. Immediately after the Civil War, the dream of many to establish museums on a par with European museums became a reality.

In 1867 Henry T. Tuckerman had pleaded for the creation of a permanent public museum of art:

> Within the last few years the advance of public taste and the increased recognition of art in this country have been among the most interesting phenomena of the times. A score of eminent and original landscape painters have achieved the highest reputations; private collections of pictures have become a new social attraction; exhibitions of works of art have grown lucrative and popular; buildings expressly for studios have been erected; sales of pictures by auction have produced unprecedented sums of money; art-shops are a delectable feature of Broadway; artist-receptions are favorite reunions of the winter; and a splendid edifice has been completed devoted to the Academy, and owing its erection to public munificence. . . . These and many other facts indicate, too plainly to be mistaken, that the time has come to establish permanent and standard galleries of art, on the most liberal scale, in our large cities.[62]

The New-York Historical Society proposed to establish such an art museum and the New York Legislature passed an act in April, 1868, setting aside a site in Central Park, covering 81st to 84th streets, west of Fifth Avenue, for use by the Society, provided that the latter construct a building at its own expense. However, grandiose architectural plans for the venture proved to be too costly and the scheme was abandoned.[63]

Meanwhile, members of the Union League Club, some of whom had been active in planning and raising funds for the Metropolitan Fair of 1864, were pressing for a metropolitan art museum. The Metropolitan Museum of Art came into being in 1870. The earliest collection of the museum's paintings rested in a brownstone at 681 Fifth Avenue and then at 128 West 14th Street before it settled in 1880 into its structure designed by Calvert Vaux at the present 82nd Street site.[64] Frank Waller's *Interior View of The Metropolitan Museum of Art When in Fourteenth Street* represents two of the galleries in the early days of the Metropolitan (*Ill. 113*).

The Whistler, the Chase, and the Waller paintings are very different in style, but they illustrate the range of "paintings of everyday life" in the late 19th century. The Whistler painting emphasizes the abstract design of the figure surrounded by Oriental motifs; the Chase picks up the glitter and color of the artist's studio; the Waller, more conservative, dwells on the anecdote of the woman absorbing knowledge of past art. All three arise from the artists' newly awakened self-consciousness of art and art history.

Even the tradition of the sporting picture was affected by the urban movement. In Thomas Eakins's *Will Schuster and Blackman Going Shooting* of 1876, Will Schuster is a city man out in the reeds hunting for rail (*Ill. 114*). As has been pointed out, Eakins nodded to the pictorial heritage of American sporting prints when he based his composition on the John Smith chromolithograph *Rail Shooting on the Delaware* of 1866[65] (*Ill. 115*). In the Smith print, the poleman is a muscular farmer with rolled-up sleeves and bare feet; the marksman is a stylishly attired but anonymous gentleman of an obviously higher social class than his guide. Schuster was a friend of Eakins, and he is appropriately but informally dressed. The black man is self-assured and serious, probably not a farmer but one of a growing

114. Thomas Eakins. *Will Schuster and Blackman Going Shooting for Rail*, 1876. Oil on canvas, 22⅛ x 30¼ inches. Yale University Art Gallery, New Haven. Bequest of Stephen Carlton Clark.

115. John Smith, Publisher. *Rail Shooting on the Delaware*, 1866. Chromolithograph, 18 x 28¼ inches. Photograph courtesy of The Old Print Shop, New York.

116. Thomas Eakins. *The Biglin Brothers Racing*, c. 1873. Oil on canvas, 24⅛ x 36⅛ inches. National Gallery of Art, Washington, D.C. Gift of Mr. and Mrs. Cornelius Vanderbilt Whitney, 1953.

number of people who depends on city sportsmen for his income.

The greater number of Eakins's sporting paintings are those depicting his friends and acquaintances rowing on the Schuylkill River, which twists through Philadelphia on its way to the Delaware River. The rowers in their sculls and pair-oared shells concentrate on the sport with the precision of professionals, as in *The Biglin Brothers Racing* of about 1873 (*Ill. 116*). Again, the figures are not of the frontier or the backwoods like those in the sporting paintings of Arthur Fitzwilliam Tait and William Ranney, but city dwellers on their day off.

Eakins peopled his paintings with serious sports-

men. More popular subjects for other artists in the postwar years were the lighter sports, such as croquet and ocean bathing. In the early 1860s Winslow Homer had designed woodcuts of skaters for *Harper's Weekly* and *Frank Leslie's Illustrated Newspaper*. After the war his designs of figures at the beach, particularly his paintings of Long Branch, New Jersey, corresponded with the upsurge of summer homes being built in the early 1870s.

Homer's *Croquet Players* of 1865 represents the popular summer sport (*Colorplate 5*). The painting compares with Eastman Johnson's *Hollyhocks* of 1876 (*Ill. 117*); the sunlight filling both paintings brings out the bright local colors. In the Johnson

painting, however, the women's faces are rendered with a soft precision that differentiates them from the other forms in the painting. Homer, on the other hand, depersonalizes the figures, concentrating instead on the flat, abstract patterns of hoops and skirts, and shadows on the lawn. Despite the contrast of their styles, the shared concern of both Johnson and Homer was to present urbanites on a holiday.

William Merritt Chase painted many works in the 1880s of figures outdoors, in the city parks, or in the sand dunes at Shinnecock, Long Island, where Chase summered. In *The Open Air Breakfast,* painted about 1888, Chase presents his wife and baby and two other relatives, posed in a brightly lit but shadowless enclosure (*Ill. 118*). The exotic touches include a 17th-century Dutch-style hat, a Japanese screen, and a Russian hound sleeping lazily on the grass. His *Central Park* of about 1887–91 depicts white-frocked, carefree city children racing around Central Park's Boat Basin (*Ill. 119*). The world of Chase and his circle was one untouched by commerce or industrialism.

Grown-ups' play included promenading on foot or in carriages in order to display their taste for elegant clothes and fine horses. In 1879 Thomas Eakins was commissioned by Fairman Rogers, the wealthy son of a Philadelphia iron merchant, to paint *Fairman Rogers Four-in-Hand* (*Ill. 120*). Eakins made nu-

117. Eastman Johnson. *Hollyhocks,* 1876. Oil on canvas, 25 x 31 inches. The New Britain Museum of American Art, New Britain, Connecticut. Harriet R. Stanley Fund.

118. William Merritt Chase. *The Open Air Breakfast,* c. 1888. Oil on canvas, 37½ x 56¾ inches. The Toledo Museum of Art, Toledo, Ohio. Gift of Florence Scott Libbey, 1953.

119. William Merritt Chase. *Central Park,* c. 1887–91. Oil on canvas, 16 x 24 inches. Mann Galleries, Miami.

merous studies of the horses, the site, and Mr. Rogers's family and servants before commencing the painting. The details of the carriage, harnesses, and dress of the participants were all meticulously recorded and set against a blaze of dark green spring foliage. In a lighter key is Frederick Childe Hassam's *Le Jour du Grand Prix* of 1888 (*Ill. 121*). Wealth proved to be international, and American painters and their well-to-do patrons went abroad. The Hassam painting records a day in Paris in late June when the leisure classes made their way to the horse races held at Longchamps.

Travel to scenic spots within the Continent and to foreign cities was a popular theme for artists in the post-Civil War years. In the early 1870s William Cullen Bryant published *Picturesque America,* an elaborate picture book advertising the scenic wonders of America. Landscape painters such as Albert Bierstadt, Thomas Hill, Sanford Gifford, Worthington Whittredge, and Thomas Moran traveled to the West, where they painted the Rocky Mountains, the Sierra Range, and the glorious California scenery.[66] In 1874 William Hahn, who had recently moved to California, painted *Yosemite Valley from Glacier Point,* which depicts a party of tourists viewing the natural splendors (*Ill. 122*). In the East Winslow Homer painted tourists in the White Mountains of New Hampshire.

But domestic excursions did not have the fascination of European travel. Henry Bacon, who had frequently sailed to the Continent, painted several shipboard scenes in the late 1870s, emphasizing anecdotal activities on deck. In his *First Sight of Land* of 1877, a young woman has cast aside her French novel and rises from her deck chair to see the stretch of land in the distance (*Ill. 123*). Julius L. Stewart enlarges the scene in *The Yacht Namouna in Venetian Waters* of 1890, where idle passengers occupy their time in reading, flirting, and talking (*Ill. 124*).

John Singer Sargent, one of a number of talented expatriates living abroad in the 1870s and 1880s, painted most of his scenes of daily life in Europe. In Sargent's *In the Luxembourg Gardens* of 1879, the wide expanse of the pavement, the silver-yellow moon, and its reflections in the pond create abstract patterns of grays and yellows (*Ill. 125*). The detail of

the glowing cigarette interrupts the scene with the discreteness of a firefly on a July night.

To the painter of the leisure classes, "daily" life became a rich woman's world of tea time, of supervising the servants (who in turn minded the children), of writing letters and reading novels, and of idling away the hours doing nothing. In these paintings women led passive existences, listening and waiting among the beautiful surroundings of French furniture, patterned wallpaper, china cups, silks, and flowers. It was not necessarily the case that the lifestyles of women had changed, but merely that artists preferred to view them in a new way. To these artists the mood evoked by a painting became more important than moralization or the representation of action.[67]

The mother in William Henry Lippincott's *Infantry in Arms* of 1887 delegates many of her responsibilities to her servants (*Ill. 126*). Attired in a dressing gown of exquisite workmanship and surrounded by handsome children and furniture, she supervises the young nurse holding the baby of the house.

Mary Cassatt, known for her ties with European Impressionism and her stunning studies of women and children, also painted women keeping company with each other. Her *A Cup of Tea* of about 1880, painted in the spatially compressed style of the Impressionists, with the figures flattened between chintz-covered settee and silver tea service, represents the gentility of well-to-do Americans in Paris (*Ill. 127*). In Cassatt's *The Loge* of about 1882, two beautiful young women passively watch the entertainment proceeding below them (*Ill. 128*). *Idle Hours* of 1888 by Julian Alden Weir is a typical title for such paintings of languid women dressed in white (*Ill. 129*).

Doing nothing was a mark of status according to Thorstein Veblen in his brilliantly ironical sociological analysis of the rich, *The Theory of the Leisure Class* of 1899. He described the women of the leisure class as creatures required to consume conspicuously, but denied purposeful activity:

> She is petted, and is permitted, or even required, to consume largely and conspicuously—vicariously for her husband or other natural guardian.

120. Thomas Eakins. *The Fairman Rogers Four-in-Hand,* 1879. Oil on canvas, 24 x 36 inches. Philadelphia Museum of Art. Gift of William Alexander Dick.

121. Frederick Childe Hassam. *Le Jour du Grand Prix* (1888). Oil on canvas, 36 x 48 inches. The New Britain Museum of American Art, New Britain, Connecticut. Grace Judd Landers Fund.

122. William Hahn. *Yosemite Valley from Glacier Point,* 1874. Oil on canvas, 27¼ x 46¼ inches. California Historical Society, San Francisco.

99

100

123. Henry Bacon. *First Sight of Land*, 1877. Oil on canvas, 28½ x 19⅝ inches. Collection of Mr. and Mrs. John I. H. Baur, Katonah, New York.

Colorplate 5. Winslow Homer. *Croquet Players,* 1865. Oil on canvas, 16 x 26 inches. Albright-Knox Art Gallery, Buffalo, New York. Charles Clifton and James G. Forsyth Funds, 1941.

Colorplate 6. William McGregor Paxton. *The New Necklace,* 1910. Oil on canvas, 35½ x 28⅛ inches. Museum of Fine Arts, Boston. Zoe Oliver Sherman Collection.

124. Julius L. Stewart. *The Yacht Namouna in Venetian Waters,* 1890. Oil on canvas, 56 x 77 inches. Wadsworth Atheneum, Hartford, Connecticut. Ella Gallup Sumner and Mary Catlin Sumner Collection.

125. John Singer Sargent. *In the Luxembourg Gardens,* 1879. Oil on canvas, 25½ x 36 inches. Courtesy of the John G. Johnson Collection, Philadelphia.

126. William Henry Lippincott. *Infantry in Arms,* 1887. Oil on canvas, 32 x 53 inches. Pennsylvania Academy of the Fine Arts, Philadelphia. Gift of Homer F. Emens and Francis C. Jones, 1922.

127. Mary Cassatt. *A Cup of Tea,* c. 1880. Oil on canvas, 25½ x 36½ inches. Museum of Fine Arts, Boston. Maria Hopkins Fund.

128. Mary Cassatt. *The Loge,* c. 1882. Oil on canvas, 31½ x 25⅛ inches. National Gallery of Art, Washington, D.C. Chester Dale Collection, 1962.

129. Julian Alden Weir. *Idle Hours,* 1888. Oil on canvas, 51⅛ x 71¼ inches. The Metropolitan Museum of Art, New York. Gift of Several Gentlemen, 1888.

She is exempted, or debarred, from vulgarly useful employment—in order to perform leisure vicariously for the good repute of her natural (pecuniary) guardian.[68]

It was an unenviable position, and one against which middle-class suffragist women rebelled.

A group of painters most active in painting leisure-class women were the "Ten American Painters," who resigned from the Society of American Artists because of its conservative policies and began to exhibit together in 1898. The Ten were Frank Weston Benson, Joseph Rodefer De Camp, Thomas Dewing, Frederick Childe Hassam, Willard Leroy Metcalf, Robert Reid, Edward Simmons, Edmund Charles Tarbell, John Henry Twachtman, and Julian Alden Weir. Paintings by Dewing are idealized and generalized tonal visions of women, which cannot strictly be called scenes of everyday life. Other artists, such as the Boston artists Benson, Tarbell, and William McGregor Paxton painted specific scenes emphasizing the material surroundings of the figures. Benson's *Girl Playing Solitaire* of 1909 presents a woman

dressed in scintillating fabrics against a golden, Oriental screen (*Ill. 130*). Lost in her own thoughts, she could be a heroine stepped out of the pages of a Henry James novel in which subtleties of mood define the actions of the protagonists.

When the women read they turn their attention to expensive illustrated books, as in Lilian Westcott Hale's *L'Edition de Luxe* and William Worcester Churchill's *Leisure* (*Ills. 131, 132*). The reading of newspapers, a popular motif in genre paintings of men at mid-century, is unthinkable for these delicate, powerless creatures. Such paintings find their contemporary analogue in the consciously aesthetic paintings of the European Symbolists. There were differences, of course. American artists did not envision women as essentially evil, destructively sexual beings as one often finds in the work of the Norwegian Edvard Munch, the English illustrator Aubrey Beardsley, or the Austrian artist Egon Schiele. The content was similar, however; art and artifice, symbolized by the illustrated books, became a substitute for involvement with life.

106

The modish ennui of upper-class living can be seen in Edmund C. Tarbell's *The Breakfast Room,* in which a young woman pauses in her repast while her male companion works at peeling an orange. Her thoughts are unknown to the spectator; she is the persona of no known story (*Ill. 133*). Defined in terms of her men and her children, but alienated from them, nothingness becomes the essential content of her life. Across the expanse of empty space (the perimeter of which contains paintings) and through the door, a maid busies herself in the adjoining room. In most of these paintings of upper-class women only men and domestics engage in activity—but that activity is at the outer circumference of empty spaces and passive women. In Tarbell's *A Rehearsal in the Studio* of about 1904, the violinist tucked into the back corner of the room plays to quietly reflective women (*Ill. 134*).

Tarbell approaches the canons of Impressionism in his asymmetrical compositions and empty spaces, but the loose brush work tightens when rendering the contour of a porcelain bowl or the reflection on a highly polished table. The preciousness of objects becomes the content of Joseph De Camp's *The Blue Cup,* in which the young domestic worker reverently wipes the delicate cup (*Ill. 135*).

The master of delineating the material variety, abundance, and opulence of leisure-class living was the Bostonian William McGregor Paxton, whose paintings recall the artistic interiors of Jan Vermeer. In his *Woman Combing Her Hair* of 1909, the young woman with her chestnut-colored hair gazes into the mirror (*Ill. 136*). Covering the table are an array of objects; silver brushes, crystal candlesticks, and a string of pearls. Hermetically sealed from the cares of the world, the beautiful young women in *The New Necklace* and *Tea Leaves,* powdered and jeweled and dressed in fine fabrics, softly gesture and incline their heads (*Colorplate 6; Ill. 137*). The airless rooms are heavy with the smells of camphor and tea, lemons and perfumes and furniture oils. Soft translucent films of color—gray, yellow, and pink tonalities—combine with brilliant Chinese turquoise to create an exquisitely artful arrangement.

130. Frank Weston Benson. *Girl Playing Solitaire,* 1909. Oil on canvas, 50 x 40 inches. Worcester Art Museum, Worcester, Massachusetts.

131. Lilian Westcott Hale. *L'Edition de Luxe,* 1910. Oil on canvas, 23 x 15⅛ inches.
Museum of Fine Arts, Boston. Gift of Miss Mary C. Wheelwright.

132. William Worcester Churchill. *Leisure,* 1910. Oil on canvas, 30 x 25¼ inches.
Museum of Fine Arts, Boston. Gift of Gorham Hubbard.

133. Edmund C. Tarbell. *The Breakfast Room*, 1899. Oil on canvas, 25 x 30 inches. Pennsylvania Academy of the Fine Arts, Philadelphia. Gift of Mr. Clement B. Newbold, 1973.

134. Edmund C. Tarbell. *A Rehearsal in the Studio,* c. 1904. Oil on canvas, 25 x 30 inches. Worcester Art Museum, Worcester, Massachusetts. Gift of Mr. and Mrs. Henry H. Sherman.

135. Joseph Rodefer De Camp. *The Blue Cup*, 1909. Oil on canvas, 50½ x 41½ inches. Museum of Fine Arts, Boston. Gift of Edwin S. Webster, Laurence T. Webster, and Mary M. Sampson, in memory of their father, Frank G. Webster.

136. William McGregor Paxton. *Woman Combing Her Hair,* 1909. Oil on canvas, 27 x 22 inches. Collection of Mr. and Mrs. Robert Douglas Hunter, Boston. (Previously exhibited as *Girl Combing Her Hair.*)

137. William McGregor Paxton. *Tea Leaves*, 1909. Oil on canvas, 36⅛ x 28¾ inches. The Metropolitan Museum of Art, New York. Gift of George A. Hearn, 1910.

138. Winslow Homer. *The Morning Bell,* c. 1866. Oil on canvas, 24 x 38¼ inches.
Yale University Art Gallery, New Haven. Bequest of Stephen Carlton Clark.

Scenes of Working-Class Life

There was an alternative tradition. Rather than choose the idle rich as subjects for their art, some artists of the second half of the 19th century portrayed urban working men and women at their chores or at rest. William Burr had depicted working women in his unusual *The Intelligence Office* of 1844 (*Ill. 55*). About 1866 Winslow Homer painted young factory women carrying lunch pails on their way to work while the bell tolls above the factory. The factory is nestled among the trees—as was typical of many factories in New England at the time. The euphonious title, *The Morning Bell,* suggests the beginning of a pleasant day (*Ill. 138*). From contemporary accounts, however, the New England factory system was not as idyllic as its industrialists avowed. There may be some irony in Homer's point of view, for in spite of the pleasant title, there is a marked joylessness about the figures. The dog hangs its head with its tail dropped between its legs, the women at the back pause, and the one central woman proceeds as if urged on by necessity.[69]

In 1879 John George Brown painted dock workers at their lunch break in *The Longshoremen's Noon* (*Ill. 139*). The painting shows a potpourri of national types sitting in the noonday sun, surrounded by the remnants of their lunches. The opened newspaper on the dock suggests that their discussion ran to the events of the day. Young boys loiter in the background. By the 1880s Brown had become well known as a painter of sentimentalized street urchins and waifs, though he was not the first to depict young transients. David Gilmour Blythe had earlier painted *A Match Seller* depicting a pathetic young boy with a basket full of matches—a character common to American and European cities (*Ill. 140*).

In art and literature poor working children came to personify the beginning of the rags-to-riches myth. In popular literature Horatio Alger exploited the appetite of the public for success stories, even though he himself had a genuine interest in the welfare of young orphans. His novel *Ragged Dick* (1867) was the first of a long list of successful Alger books about young boys who act out the American dream of achieving material wealth and social status through thrift, cleverness, and a good measure of luck. Mr. Whitney, Dick's benefactor, encouraged the young bootblack to cultivate such virtues: "I hope, my lad . . . . you will prosper and rise in the world. You know in this free country poverty is no bar to a man's advancement."[70]

The rags-to-riches myth had a strong appeal in the years of prosperity following the Civil War, when the cleverness and individualism of men like Andrew Carnegie and John D. Rockefeller personified the dream story come true. The myth was also a powerful device to encourage the working classes to conform to the precepts of economy, hard work, thrift, and respect for authority.

The pictorial equivalents to the Alger heroes are John George Brown's well-scrubbed, well-proportioned, healthy bootblacks, match sellers, and flower girls—the city version of rural rascals. In Brown's *A Tough Story,* three bootblacks listen intently as their colleague relates a personal experience (*Ill. 141*). Brown copyrighted many of his paintings and thus realized some financial success from his illustrations.

Sentimentality is the handmaiden of hypocrisy because it permits emotional release without requiring the intellectual commitment to social or moral action. Brown's paintings reassured his patrons that life was happy, that young beggar children were well off. The stark reality and hardships of child laborers remained for the photographers—men such as Jacob Riis and Lewis Hine—to record in the 1890s and the early years of the 20th century.

About 1882 Thomas Pollock Anshutz painted *Ironworkers: Noontime* (*Ill. 142*). A student of Thomas Eakins, who himself had made extensive studies of human anatomy and the nude, Anshutz captured a number of men standing in various poses under the glare of the noonday sun. The painting is factual and objective—as might be expected of a student of Eakins. The scene includes four younger boys washing by the water pump and scampering behind the central figures. In 1880 the official statistics for children gainfully employed between the ages of ten to fifteen showed 1,118,536; by 1900, the number had

139. John George Brown. *The Longshoremen's Noon,* 1879. Oil on canvas, 33¼ x 50¼ inches.
Corcoran Gallery of Art, Washington, D.C.

140. David Gilmour Blythe. *A Match Seller*, c. 1856–65. Oil on canvas, 27 x 22 inches. North Carolina Museum of Art, Raleigh.

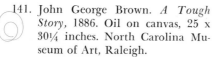141. John George Brown. *A Tough Story*, 1886. Oil on canvas, 25 x 30¼ inches. North Carolina Museum of Art, Raleigh.

117

142. Thomas Pollock Anshutz. *Ironworkers: Noontime,* c. 1882. Oil on canvas, 17 x 24 inches. Private collection, New York. Photograph courtesy of Kennedy Galleries, Inc., New York.

Colorplate 7. Robert Koehler. *The Strike*, 1886. Oil on canvas, 71½ x 108½ inches. Collection of Lee Baxandall, New York. Color photograph courtesy Local 1199, Drug and Hospital Union, New York.

Colorplate 8. John Sloan. *The Picnic Grounds*, 1906–07. Oil on canvas, 24 x 36 inches.
Whitney Museum of American Art, New York.

reached 1,750,178.[71] While the urban middle class—the subjects of Chase, Tarbell, Hassam—was getting richer, the poor seemed to get poorer. Weekly wages decreased during the 1870s, particularly after the depression of 1873; and in most poor, working families the children had to work.

Charles Frederick Ulrich's *The Village Print Shop* of about 1885 presents a young apprentice pausing from his labors to have a drink (*Ill. 143*). Ulrich presents the impersonal environment of the shop by rendering the cast-iron stove, printing materials, and the press with precision. To de-emphasize the narrative elements and reinforce the sense of the alienation of work, Ulrich obscures the faces and particularly the eyes of all three workers.

In contrast, Ulrich emphasizes the anxious and waiting eyes of foreign immigrants in his 1884 painting *In the Land of Promise—Castle Garden* (*Ill. 144*). Built about 1808 as a fort to defend New York City, Castle Garden was remodeled and became a famous amusement hall and opera house, but from 1855 to 1892 it functioned as an immigration station. The figures include many national types seated on rude benches, in the center of which sits a nursing mother, a secular Madonna image. The painting was exhibited at the National Academy of Design in 1884, the year when Frédéric Auguste Bartholdi had completed the Statue of Liberty in France. A gift from the French Government to the American people, the statue proclaimed America's mission to enlighten the world and shelter its refugees.[72]

Ulrich's realism is both formal and thematic. In order to suggest that his painting is a mere segment of a larger reality, Ulrich cuts off the figures at the periphery of the composition. Other figures, such as the child sitting on the trunk, look out to the side, their attention drawn to activities unfolding outside the confines of the canvas edge. The litter and stains on the floor negate picturesqueness. The weary but serious faces imply that the fortunes of the travelers

143. Charles Frederick Ulrich. *The Village Print Shop*, c. 1885. Oil on canvas, 23 x 23 inches. Collection of Mrs. Norman B. Woolworth, New York.

144. Charles Frederick Ulrich. *In the Land of Promise—Castle Garden*, 1884. Oil on canvas, 28⅜ x 35¾ inches. Corcoran Gallery of Art, Washington, D.C.

have not been settled; like those in Alfred Stieglitz's now famous photograph *Steerage* of 1907, they may be labeled undesirables and shipped back to Europe.[73]

In the late 1870s and throughout the 1880s there was a series of strikes across the nation, with workers demanding higher pay, shorter hours, and better working conditions. Labor leaders around the country supported the movement to make the eight-hour day the legal standard, and May 1, 1886, was chosen as the target date to achieve their goal. Workers responded, particularly in Chicago, a center of left-wing activity. On May Day a general strike began; the climax came on May 3, at the McCormick Harvester works, when the police rushed a crowd of locked-out workers, killing one and mortally wounding four or five others. To protest, the strike leaders called a rally for the following day at Chicago's Haymarket Square. By the end of the rally someone had thrown a bomb at an advancing squadron of about 280 police sent in to break up the final group of about 200 demonstrators.[74] Seven policemen were killed and others injured; the police retaliated, killing four in the crowd. In the weeks following, hysteria gripped the business community of Chicago, which demanded revenge. Eight labor leaders, some of whom were self-confessed anarchists, were charged with the murder on the grounds that they had incited the unknown bomb-thrower. Brought to trial and found guilty, seven were sentenced to death in what has come to be known as one of the most injudicious trials in American jurisprudence.[75]

Robert Koehler had shown *The Socialist* at the National Academy of Design in 1885. In the spring exhibition of 1886, he exhibited *The Strike* (*Color-plate 7*), which created an immediate sensation, particularly because of the current situation. In later years he recalled his motive for painting the work:

> *The Strike* was in my thoughts for years. It was suggested by the Pittsburgh strike [of 1877]. Its actual inception was in Munich and there the first sketches were made. I had always known the working man and with some I had been intimate. My father was a machinist and I was very much at home in the works where he was em-

ployed. Well, when the time was good and ready, I went from Munich over to England and in London and Birmingham, I made studies and sketches of the working man—his gestures, his clothes. The atmosphere and setting of the picture were done in England, as I wanted the smoke. The figures were studies from life, but were painted in Germany. Yes, I consider *The Strike* the best, that is the strongest and most individual work I have yet done.[76]

The response of artists and critics of the time was enthusiastic. The reviewer for the *New York Times,* April 4, 1886, described the work at length, admiring the realism but deploring as excessive the inclusion of the woman, baby, and beggar girl:

> Mr. Koehler has done well to show the earnest group of sweating workmen, quite possibly with justice on their side, but ready, some of them, to take the law in their own hands.

> He has contrasted with them fairly well the prim capitalist. But in trying to rouse our sympathies with a beggar woman his moral gets heavy. . . .

> All the same, "The Strike" is the most significant work of this Spring exhibition.[77]

The painting, with all its didacticism, seems to be one of the first to depict not just the dignity of labor, which was exemplified by John Ferguson Weir's *Forging the Shaft* of 1877 (*Ill. 145*), but the struggle of the working classes against the industrialists and capitalists. Koehler's work was reproduced as the center spread of *Harper's Weekly* on the very week of May 1, 1886. Later the painting received honorable mention at the Paris Exposition Universelle of 1889. Although the painting was bought by the city of Minneapolis, it apparently was unappreciated by the town fathers and was virtually forgotten. Representations of the striking proletariat were perhaps too dangerous and subversive; most patrons preferred paintings of small shopkeepers by such artists as Jefferson David Chalfant and Louis Charles Moeller.

145. John Ferguson Weir. *Forging the Shaft* (1877). Oil on canvas, 52¹⁄₁₆ x 73¼ inches. The Metropolitan Museum of Art, New York. Gift of Lyman G. Bloomingdale, 1901.

Early 20th-Century Realism

In Philadelphia in the mid-1890s, a number of young artist-illustrators of the next generation—William J. Glackens, George Luks, Everett Shinn, and John Sloan—turned their attention to the social circumstances of working people. They had all worked for *The Philadelphia Press* and were drawn to the robust personality of Robert Henri, an older Philadelphia artist then teaching at the Pennsylvania Academy of the Fine Arts. Henri's art had developed from the teaching of Thomas Anshutz and he had some Paris training; in style Henri's quick bravura technique was close to that of the Munich-trained portrait painter Frank Duveneck. Henri was a welcome antidote to the aestheticism of The Ten and the academic Beaux Arts style of such artists as George de Forest Brush and Abbott Thayer. When Henri moved to New York City in 1904, the younger artists, some of whom had already moved to New York, collected around him. Henri influenced them toward a realism shaped less by the political radicalism, which characterized the writers of the time—Hamlin Garland, Jack London, Stephen Crane, Frank Norris,

and Theodore Dreiser—than by an appreciation of the sheer energy of the modern city and the working people who gave it pulse. Henri exhorted:

> As I see it, there is only one reason for the development of art in America, and that is that the people of America learn the means of expressing themselves in their own time and in their own land. In this country we have no need of art as a culture; no need of art as a refined and elegant performance; no need for art for poetry's sake, or any of these things for their own sake. What we do need is art that expresses the *spirit* of the people of today.[78]

In attempting to capture that spirit these artists searched for new subject matter. As artist-journalists Luks, Glackens, Sloan, and Shinn were accustomed to looking at urban life about them—catching the gestures and momentary expressions of life. They embraced New York with enthusiasm. They eschewed upper-class ladies reclining in wicker chairs, selecting instead the city streets, robust children playing, grown-ups strolling in parks and frolicking on the public beaches, or visiting the theaters and sporting events. Exhibiting together for the first time at the Macbeth Galleries in 1908, they were immediately nicknamed The Eight because the exhibition also included Ernest Lawson, Arthur B. Davies, and Maurice Prendergast. But it was the realists of the exhibition—Henri, Glackens, Luks, Shinn, and Sloan—who stunned the public with their vibrant, life-oriented painting. Other painters followed their lead, including George Bellows, Jerome Myers, Eugene Higgins, and Glenn O. Coleman, and the group as a whole came to be known as the Ashcan School.

Fascinated with the building activity progressing in New York, George Bellows painted scenes of workers drilling into the rock of Manhattan at the excavation site of Pennsylvania Station and building the skyscrapers which were to become the symbol of New York (*Ill. 147*). Frederick Childe Hassam was similarly caught up in the rhythm of the city when he painted *The Hovel and the Skyscraper* in 1904 (Collection of Mr. and Mrs. Meyer P. Potamkin).

George Luks, a self-styled pugilist, sometime coal miner, and newspaperman rejected his bourgeois origins and identified himself with the struggles of the working classes. Rather than paint New York's elegant avenues and parks, he turned to the Lower East Side. His *Hester Street* of 1905 captures the bustle of pushcarts, vendors, shoppers, con artists, and children (*Ill. 148*).

Jerome Myers was also associated with the group. Although he experienced poverty in his early years, his art was without bitterness and rancor. He portrayed groups of working-class New Yorkers attending summer revival meetings, sitting in front of their tenements, or waiting for the ferry on a summer night, as in *At the Ferry Slip* of 1905 (*Ill. 149*).

William Glackens's paintings also capture the life of the city, but the figures are rarely poor. Exuberant children playing in Central Park, dressed in sailor suits in the summer and rabbit fur in the winter, inhabit his paintings (*Ills. 150, 151*). The youth, the energy, and the potential for growth of children symbolized life and optimism. With exuberance, the children in George Luks's *The Spielers* of 1905 and George Bellows's *Kids* of 1906 captured a democratic and lusty spirit of communal activity (*Frontispiece; Ill. 152*).

Younger than the painters of The Eight, George Bellows represented the personification of heroic and masculine determination. His realism was one of physical action. Bellows's *Stag at Sharkey's* of 1907 was painted only a few years after Thomas Eakins's *Between Rounds* of 1899 (*Ills. 153, 154*). Both are concerned with the subject of the masculine boxing match. Eakins selects the moment of rest and of psychological reflection. To the older artist, boxing was a contest of skill and strategy, akin to the Greek games. Bellows chooses the moment of physical contact—the faces of the boxers are obscured—and the viewer sees diagonal flashes of muscular flesh. To Bellows, realism concerned itself with the physical facts of existence, the actions of men and women rather than their intentions.

Together with sporting events, the color and activity of the theater attracted many early realists; in fact, amateur theatricals and costume parties seem to have been part of the student life at Henri's Phila-

146. Robert Henri. *West 57th Street, N.Y.*, 1902. Oil on canvas, 26 x 32 inches. Yale University Art Gallery, New Haven. The Mabel Brady Garvan Collection.

147. George Bellows. *Pennsylvania Station Excavation,* 1909. Oil on canvas, 30¼ x 38¼ inches. The Brooklyn Museum. A. Augustus Healy Fund.

148. George M. Luks. *Hester Street* (1905). Oil on canvas, 26 x 35¹³/₁₆ inches. The Brooklyn Museum. Dick S. Ramsay Fund.

149. Jerome Myers. *At the Ferry Slip,* 1905. Oil on canvas, 25¼ x 30¼ inches. The Metropolitan Museum of Art, New York. Purchase, George A. Hearn Fund, 1966.

150. William J. Glackens. *Central Park in Winter,* c. 1905. Oil on canvas, 25 x 30 inches. The Metropolitan Museum of Art, New York. George A. Hearn Fund, 1921.

151. William J. Glackens. *Maypole, Central Park,* 1905. Oil on canvas, 25⅛ x 30 inches. The Fine Arts Museums of San Francisco. Gift of the de Young Museum Society and the Charles E. Merrill Trust Fund.

152. George Bellows. *Kids,* 1906. Oil on canvas, 32 x 42 inches.
Private collection, New York.

153. Thomas Eakins. *Between Rounds,* 1899. Oil on canvas, 50¼ x 40 inches. Philadelphia Museum of Art. Gift of Mrs. Thomas Eakins and Miss Mary A. Williams.

154. George Bellows. *Stag at Sharkey's,* 1907. Oil on canvas, 36¼ x 48¼ inches. The Cleveland Museum of Art. Hinman B. Hurlbut Collection.

155. William J. Glackens. *Hammerstein's Roof Garden*, c. 1903. Oil on canvas, 30 x 25 inches. Whitney Museum of American Art, New York.

delphia studio. During the 1890s theater personalities such as Maude Adams, Diamond Jim Brady, Lillian Russell, and Florenz Ziegfeld, Jr., fascinated an audience of New Yorkers. Interest in the theater was international, however, and Glackens's *Hammerstein's Roof Garden* of about 1903 (*Ill. 155*) finds its European equivalent in the works of the English artist Walter Sickert and the French Impressionist Edgar Degas. Everett Shinn, one of the least-known of The Eight, painted a number of scenes of trapeze artists and pretty actresses posed at the footlights, as, for example, his *Revue* of 1908 (*Ill. 156*).

John Sloan, the most talented artist of this group, united a broad range of novel subject matter with brilliant technical ability. Like the others, he began as an artist-reporter for *The Philadelphia Press.*

His Art Nouveau poster-style graphics, newspaper illustrations, and cartoons would alone assure his place in the history of turn-of-the-century graphics. But when painting he exchanged the sinuous line, sharp silhouette, and textureless surfaces of Art Nouveau for heavy forms, painterly edges, and an impasto surface. His subjects were reportorial rather than art historical—drawn from the topical occurrences that he daily observed. Sloan noted in his diary of June 5, 1907: "Walked up to Henri's studio. On the way saw a humorous sight of interest. A window, low, second story, bleached blond hairdresser bleaching the hair of a client. A small interested crowd about."[79] The painting produced, *Hairdresser's Window*, is a vivid transcription of that witnessed event (*Ill. 157*).

156. Everett Shinn. *Revue,* 1908. Oil on canvas, 18 x 24 inches. Whitney Museum of American Art, New York.

Henri must have felt great affection for his younger colleague, who seemed to epitomize the artist of the new age. Henri later said of Sloan:

The artists who produce the most satisfactory art are in my mind those who are absorbed in the civilization in which they are living. . . . John Sloan, with his demand for the rights of man, and his love of the people; his keen observation of the people's folly, his knowledge of their virtues and his surpassing interest in all things. I never met Sloan but what he had something new to tell me of some vital thing in life that interested him, and which probably was eventually typified in his work.[80]

Sloan's keen eye for the life around him was fortified by his social conscience. Of all The Eight he was the artist most overtly political. He joined the Socialist Party in 1910 and was the Socialist Party candidate for the New York State Assembly in November of that year. By 1912 he had become acting art editor of *The Masses*. He also contributed to other Socialist publications, such as *The Call*. His graphic sketches and drawings of working women, strikers, retaliating policemen, courtroom lawyers, and corpulent capitalists were moving indictments of the class system in America. Sloan's witty *Gray and Brass* of 1907 is a translation into oil painting of his social commentary (*Ill. 158*). The pugnacious plutocrat and

157. John Sloan. *Hairdresser's Window*, 1907. Oil on canvas, 31⅞ x 26 inches. Wadsworth Atheneum, Hartford, Connecticut. Ella Gallup Sumner and Mary Catlin Sumner Collection.

158. John Sloan. *Gray and Brass* (1907). Oil on canvas, 22 x 27 inches. Collection of Arthur G. Altschul, New York.

his entourage of haughty women (the young one ignoring the advances of a strolling sailor) are far different from the elegantly attired, sympathetically rendered figures in Eakins's *Fairman Rogers Four-in-Hand (Ill. 120)*. Sloan much preferred the honesty of young working-class people making use of the public facilities in *South Beach Bathers* of 1908 and *The Picnic Grounds* of 1906–7 (*Ill. 159; Colorplate 8*).

In the second decade of the century, the talented artists of the next generation returned to a preoccupation with aesthetic problems—not consciously aesthetic subject matter such as ladies on lawn chairs but rather aesthetic formal concerns. The turn toward involvement with the internal, abstract elements of painting was brought on in part by the excitement of the new techniques and styles of Cubism. But it was also part of the disillusionment and cynicism of artists immediately before and during World War I about the possibilities of subject matter as a vehicle for social change. In the decade of the 1930s, the Social Realists returned to the conditions and experiences of the urban working class for themes for their art and plunged into social issues more radical than their predecessors.

159. John Sloan. *South Beach Bathers,* 1908. Oil on canvas, 25⅞ x 31⅞ inches. Walker Art Center, Minneapolis.

A Century in Retrospect

The earliest genre paintings in America were close to their English and European prototypes—paintings of village inns and country dances. But nationalism and idealism urged American artists to paint scenes that would touch the patriotic hearts of their patrons. When Americans idealized the native yeoman, artists responded by painting the farmer and his family at work and at rest. Indeed, the agrarian myth of the rugged, hardworking farmer continued to hold the attention of painters long after the locus of politics and government had shifted to the cities.

In the post-Civil War years of rapid industrialization, painters turned to subjects which appealed to an increasingly prosperous, more sophisticated, middle class—subjects of urban ladies and gentlemen promenading in city parks, relaxing at summer resorts, or listening to music in well-appointed parlors. The end of the Gilded Age saw paintings of a select, élite way of life, paintings that emphasized the sumptuous materiality of wealthy homes.

Given the social and economic circumstances of most Americans and the growing critical literature of protest, a reaction toward the aesthetic preciousness and pretentiousness of these paintings was inevitable. A group of Philadelphia artist-reporters rejected the relevance of swooning, pearl-laden gentlewomen and turned their attention to the life of the city streets—vendors, hairdressers, and working-class picnickers. Nevertheless, most American scenes of everyday life done between 1810 and 1910, whether of working farmers or strolling shopgirls, were painted with a large measure of optimism and affection.

Genre paintings are paintings of everyday life. But painters are highly selective in the choice of the life they render. Any definition of "genre painting" that seeks to limit it to a time and place, or which confines it to the subject matter and criteria relevant to earlier generations, fails to explain the reasons why an artist was innovative, or why he relied upon traditional solutions.

By the large, the painters' America represented neither conditions nor events, neither the typical nor the specific, but an artful blend of fact and fantasy, of realities and dreams. The genre painting that has survived and has been treasured reassured its select audience of a continuity between the past and the present. But the paintings did not simply serve their patrons as a nostalgic respite from the pressures of the day. Widely exhibited and reproduced, many also contributed to and perpetuated nationalistic and élitist attitudes which are with us still.

Notes

1. These views included local urban landmarks animated by figures. Thomas Birch later included in his landscapes staffage figures based on designs from William H. Pyne's *Etchings of Rustic Figures, for the Embellishment of Landscape* (London, 1815). See Doris J[ean] Creer, "Thomas Birch: A Study of the Condition of Painting and the Artist's Position in Federal America" (master's thesis, University of Delaware, 1958).
2. G.M., "Review of the Second Annual Exhibition," *The Port Folio* [Series 3] VIII: 1 (July, 1812), 24. See also Milo M[erle] Naeve, "John Lewis Krimmel: His Life, His Art, and His Critics" (master's thesis, University of Delaware, 1955).
3. "Explanation of the Plates," *The Analectic Magazine*, (New Series) I: 1 (February, 1820), 175.
4. According to Naeve, *op. cit.*, p. 170, Mount must have known of the painting itself, because George Lehman, who copied the design, did not work with Cephas G. Childs of Philadelphia until 1835–36. See also Naeve, *op. cit.*, p. 184.
5. William Sidney Mount, "Whitney Journal," Suffolk Museum & Carriage House, Stony Brook, New York.
6. Mount described the spectator as a farmer; in his Diary, July 21, 1838, he noted: "I am painting a picture representing a painter showing his picture to a country man—farmer. It is thought to be my best." See Alfred Frankenstein, *Painter of Rural America: William Sidney Mount 1807–1868* (Stony Brook, New York: Suffolk Museum & Carriage House, 1968).
7. Mount, "Whitney Journal," entry dated February, 1854.
8. Mount, "Whitney Journal," entry dated January 18, 1850.
9. Mount resented the miserly patron. In one passage, dated September 26, 1850, "Whitney Journal," he remarks: "I do not approve of our best pictures being owned by misers—so that artists must take a note and his hat under his arm before he can have a sight of some favorite picture. The best works should be obtained and placed in some public Gallery for the benefit of Amateurs and artists." Many museum curators in our present time have experienced the same difficulties in viewing historically famous paintings in private collections.
10. Artists of the period preoccupied with representing emotional states through facial expressions were aided by a number of books on expression, such as Johann Caspar Lavater's *Essays on Physiognomy,* the first American edition of which appeared in Boston in the 1790s. See E. Maurice Bloch, *George Caleb Bingham: The Evolution of an Artist* (Berkeley and Los Angeles: University of California Press, 1967), p. 133.
11. See Jules David Prown, "Washington Irving's Interest in Art and His Influence upon American Painting" (master's thesis, University of Delaware, 1956).
12. See Edward Pessen, *Jacksonian America: Society, Personality and Politics* (Homewood, Illinois: Dorsey Press, 1969), pp. 5–38.
13. Mount, "Whitney Journal," entry dated September 15, 1850.
14. For the influence of Ruskin in America, see Roger B. Stein, *John Ruskin and Aesthetic Thought in America, 1840–1900* (Cambridge, Massachusetts: Harvard University Press, 1967).
15. This essay will not deal with the pioneer and the frontier as subjects for genre painters; for a discussion of those themes, see Patricia Hills, *The American Frontier: Images and Myths* (New York: Whitney Museum of American Art, 1973).
16. Ralph Waldo Emerson, "The American Scholar," *The Works of Ralph Waldo Emerson*, ed. J. E. Cabot

(Boston and New York, 1883), I, 110–11. Much of the following discussion of nationalism was developed in the author's doctoral dissertation, "The Genre Painting of Eastman Johnson: The Sources and Development of His Style and Themes," 2 vols. (New York University, 1973).

17. *Op. cit.,* "The Poet," III, 40–41.
18. See Benjamin T. Spencer, *The Quest for Nationality* (Syracuse, New York: Syracuse University Press, 1957), p. 86.
19. G*******, "The Prairie on Fire," *The Garland for 1830: Designed as a Christmas and New-Year's Present* (New York: Josiah Drake, 1830), 150–52. See also Benjamin Rowland, Jr., "Popular Romanticism: Art and the Gift Books," *The Art Quarterly,* XX (Winter, 1957), 374.
20. Quoted in Spencer, *op. cit.,* p. 146.
21. Quoted in Spencer, *op. cit.,* p. 70.
22. *Bulletin of the American Art-Union,* 1849, unpaged. For a discussion of the American Art-Union, see Charles E. Baker, "The American Art-Union," in Mary Bartlett Cowdrey, *The American Academy of Fine Arts and American Art-Union,* 2 vols. (New York: The New-York Historical Society, 1953), I, 95–240.
23. Quoted in Baker, *op. cit.,* I, 152.
24. *Bulletin of the American Art-Union,* 1849, unpaged.
25. See Pessen, *op. cit.,* pp. 5–38.
26. "American Painters: Their Errors as Regards Nationality," *Cosmopolitan Art Journal,* I, No. 4 (June, 1857), 116.
27. See pp. 70–76 for further discussion of explicitly nostalgic paintings.
28. Henry T. Tuckerman, *Book of the Artists: American Artist Life, Comprising Biographical and Critical Sketches of American Artists, Preceded by an Historical Account of the Rise and Progress of Art in America,* 2 vols. (New York: James F. Carr, 1967), p. 471. (First published in 1867.)
29. For a discussion of the Deas and Matteson paintings, see Ellwood Parry, *The Image of the Indian and the Black Man in American Art, 1590–1900* (New York: George Braziller, Inc., 1974), pp. 77–81.
30. I am grateful to William H. Gerdts for bringing the Beard painting to my attention.
31. See Lorenz Eitner, "The Open Window and the Storm-tossed Boat: An Essay in the Iconography of Romanticism," *Art Bulletin,* XXXVII (December, 1957), 279–90.
32. See Frank Luther Mott, *A History of American Magazines,* 5 vols., I (1741–1850) (Cambridge, Massachusetts: The Belknap Press of the Harvard University Press, 1957), pp. 500–594.
33. See Richard N. Current, T. Harry Williams, and

Frank Freidel, *American History: A Survey,* 3d ed. (New York: Alfred A. Knopf, 1971), pp. 284, 864.
34. Current, Williams, and Freidel, *op. cit.,* p. 284.
35. See George Rogers Taylor, *The Transportation Revolution, 1815–1860* (New York: Harper & Row, 1968), p. 85. (First published in 1951.)
36. See Bloch, *op. cit.,* pp. 128–68.
37. Bloch, *op. cit.,* p. 133.
38. See Robert F. Westervelt, "The Whig Painter of Missouri," *The American Art Journal,* II, No. 1 (Spring, 1970), pp. 46–53. The Locofocos grew from a New York reform faction of the Democratic Party. The name came from "locofoco" matches, which were used to light a meeting hall in 1835, when the regular, Tammany Democrats had turned off the gas.
39. Frances Trollope, *Domestic Manners of the Americans* (New York: Vintage Books, 1960), p. 222. (First published in 1832.)
40. See Parry, *op. cit.,* p. 97.
41a. Harriet Beecher Stowe, *Uncle Tom's Cabin* (New York: New American Library, 1966), p. 109. (First published in 1851–52.)
41b. Stowe, *op. cit.,* pp. 349–50.
42. Eyre Crowe, *With Thackeray in America* (London: Cassell and Company Limited, 1893), pp. 132–33.
43. Crowe, *op. cit.,* p. 134.
44. Quoted in David H. Wallace, *John Rogers: The People's Sculptor* (Middletown, Connecticut: Wesleyan University Press, 1967), p. 183.
45. Tuckerman, *Book of the Artists,* p. 470.
46. Quoted in Thomas S. Cummings, *Historic Annals of The National Academy of Design* (Philadelphia: George W. Childs, Publisher, 1865), p. 301.
47. See Lloyd Goodrich, *The Graphic Art of Winslow Homer* (New York: The Museum of Graphic Art, 1968), plates 13–20. In 1864 Homer did a series for Prang entitled *Life in Camp,* twenty-four postcard-size lithographs; see Goodrich, *op. cit.,* plates 21–24.
48. Tuckerman, *Book of the Artists,* p. 450.
49. See John Wilmerding, *Winslow Homer* (New York: Praeger Publishers, 1972), for examples of Homer's Civil War sketches and paintings and contemporary photographs.
50. See Hills, "The Genre Painting of Eastman Johnson . . . ," *op. cit.* p. 80.
51. Mark Twain and Charles Dudley Warner, *The Gilded Age: A Tale of Today* (New York: The New American Library, 1969), pp. 137–38. (First published in 1873.)
52. Henry T. Tuckerman, "Children," *The Galaxy,* IV (1867), 318.
53. *Ibid.,* p. 320.
54. Eugene Benson, "Childhood in Modern Literature," *Appleton's Journal,* I (April 24, 1869), 118–20.

55. The chromo is reproduced in Katharine Morrison McClinton, *The Chromolithographs of Louis Prang* (New York: Clarkson N. Potter, Inc., 1973), p. 10.

56. G[eorge] W. Sheldon, *American Painters: With Eighty-three Examples of Their Work Engraved on Wood* (New York: D. Appleton and Company, 1879), p. 29.

57. Lizzie W. Champney, "The Summer Haunts of American Artists," *The Century Magazine*, XXX, No. 5 (September, 1885), 854.

58. See Harold L. Peterson, *Americans at Home: From the Colonists to the Late Victorians* (New York: Charles Scribner's Sons, 1971), plate 126.

59. See Susan J. Clarke, "A Chapter in East Meets West: The Japanese Print and the Work of John La Farge, William Morris Hunt, and Winslow Homer, 1858–1870" (master's thesis, University of Michigan, 1973), p. 4, and Ruth Berenson Katz, "John La Farge as Painter and Critic" (Ph.D. dissertation, Radcliffe College, 1951), pp. 60–63.

60. Cummings, *op. cit.*, p. 285. The Japanese turned down the invitation.

61. Russell Sturgis, *The Galaxy*, IV (1867), 230.

62. Tuckerman, *Book of the Artists*, p. 12.

63. R. W. G. Vail, *Knickerbocker Birthday: A Sesquicentennial History of The New-York Historical Society, 1804–1954* (New York: The New-York Historical Society, 1954), p. 119.

64. Leo Lerman, *The Museum: One Hundred Years and The Metropolitan Museum of Art* (New York: The Viking Press, 1969), p. 52.

65. The source of the Eakins painting was first brought to the author's attention by a lecture delivered by David Sellin at the College Art Association Annual Meeting held in January, 1972. See also Ellwood C. Parry III and Maria Chamberlin-Hellman, "Thomas Eakins as an Illustrator, 1878–1881," *The American Art Journal* V, No. 1 (May, 1973), 20–45.

66. Many of the landscape artists contributed to the national parks movement by exhibiting their paintings of American scenic wonders and therefore rallying public opinion. See William H. Truettner and Robin Bolton-Smith, *National Parks and the American Landscape* (Washington, D.C.: National Collection of Fine Arts, Smithsonian Institution, 1972). Photography was, of course, an aid to almost all these landscape painters.

67. For a discussion of American painters concerned with the evocation of mood, see Wanda M. Corn, *The Color of Mood: American Tonalism, 1880–1910* (San Francisco: M. H. de Young Memorial Museum and the California Palace of the Legion of Honor, 1972).

68. Thorstein Veblen, *The Theory of the Leisure Class: An Economic Study of Institutions* (New York: The New American Library, 1953), p. 232. (First published in 1899.)

69. Line engravings of designs made by Homer of women factory workers were reproduced in *Harper's Weekly* in the issues of July 25, 1868, and December 13, 1873.

70. Horatio Alger, Jr., *Ragged Dick and Mark, The Match Boy* (New York: Collier Books, 1962), p. 108. (*Ragged Dick* was first published in 1867.)

71. Fred A. Shannon, *The Centennial Years: A Political and Economic History of America from the Late 1870s to the Early 1890s,* ed. Robert Huhn Jones (Garden City, Long Island: Anchor Books, 1969), p. 203. (First published by Doubleday & Company, Inc., 1967.)

72. See Benjamin Levine and Isabelle F. Story, *Statue of Liberty* (Washington, D.C.: National Park Service Historical Handbook Series No. 11, 1952). The poet Emma Lazarus wrote a sonnet to the statue in 1883, which goes in part:

"Keep ancient lands, your storied pomp!" cries she
With silent lips. "Give me your tired, your poor,
Your huddled masses yearning to breathe free
The wretched refuse of your teeming shore.
Send these, the homeless, tempest-tost to me,
I lift my lamp beside the golden door!"

73. See Dorothy Norman, *Alfred Stieglitz: An American Seer* (New York: Random House, 1960), p. 75, for the circumstances of Stieglitz's photographing the scene.

74. Shannon, *op. cit.*, p. 238.

75. *Ibid.*, p. 239. See also Current, Williams, and Freidel, *op. cit.*, p. 457. Of the seven, four were hung, two had their sentences commuted to life imprisonment, and one allegedly committed suicide in his cell.

76. R. Koehler, *The Journal*, Minneapolis, March 23, 1901, Part II, p. 10. I am grateful to Lee Baxandall, the present owner of *The Strike*, for putting his research at my disposal. My thanks also to Moe Foner, Executive Secretary of Local 1199, Drug and Hospital Union, for his assistance in transporting the painting from the 1199 Gallery, 310 West 43d Street, where it is usually on view, to the Whitney exhibition.

77. *The New York Times*, April 4, 1886, p. 4.

78. Robert Henri, "The New York Exhibition of Independent Artists," *Craftsman*, XVIII, No. 2 (1910), as quoted in Barbara Rose, *Readings in American Art Since 1900: A Documentary Survey* (New York: Frederick A. Praeger, 1968), pp. 39–40.

79. Quoted in David W. Scott and E. John Bullard, *John Sloan: 1871–1951* (Washington, D.C.: National Gallery of Art, 1971), p. 98.

80. Henri, *op. cit.*, quoted in Rose, *op. cit.*, pp. 40–41.

Selected Biographies

Compiled by Mehrnoz Mahmudian and Peninah Petruck

Washington Allston was born in Georgetown, South Carolina, on November 5, 1779. He grew up in Newport, Rhode Island, and graduated from Harvard in 1800, where he received honors in both poetry and painting. The following year he sailed for England. He studied with Benjamin West and then toured Europe to study the old masters. In 1808 Allston returned to Boston. In 1811 he went back to England with his wife and his pupil, Samuel F. B. Morse. He returned in 1818, probably due to financial difficulties, and spent the rest of his days in the secluded company of select friends, trying to recreate the art and atmosphere of Europe and working painstakingly at his biblical painting *Belshazzar's Feast*. Although his romantic and poetic paintings became unfashionable, he was nevertheless an influential figure in the Boston art world, encouraging many of the younger artists. Allston died on July 9, 1843, in Cambridgeport, Massachusetts.

Thomas Pollock Anshutz was born in Newport, Kentucky, on October 5, 1851, and grew up in Wheeling, an Ohio River town. In 1873 he studied briefly at the National Academy of Design in New York. He was a pupil of Thomas Eakins and Christian Schussele at the Pennsylvania Academy of the Fine Arts in Philadelphia in 1875, and within six years became a member of the faculty. Anshutz studied at the Académie Julian in Paris in 1892. Within a year he returned to Philadelphia and resumed his professorship at the Pennsylvania Academy, succeeding William Merritt Chase as head of the faculty in 1909. Famous as a teacher, Anshutz played an important role in transmitting the theories of Eakins to future generations. Among his pupils were such accomplished artists as William Glackens, Robert Henri, George Luks, and John Sloan. Anshutz died in Fort Washington, Pennsylvania, on June 16, 1912.

John Antrobus was born in Warwickshire, England, about 1837. A poet, portraitist, and genre painter, he came to the United States, advertising his talents first in Montgomery, Alabama, 1855, and in New Orleans, 1860. Antrobus was painting scenes of plantation life in the South when, at the start of the Civil War, he was commissioned as a lieutenant in the Delhi Southrons and left for Virginia in July, 1861. Moving north after the war, he lived in Chicago and Washington before he settled in Detroit in 1875. Antrobus became a popular artist, frequently contributing to the local newspapers. He died in Detroit on October 18, 1907.

Henry Bacon was born on September 10, 1839, in Haverhill, Massachusetts. Like many American painters of his day, he was an illustrator. Enlisting in the Army in 1847, Bacon later served as a field artist during the Civil War. He studied in Europe—specifically in Dresden and in Paris under Cabanel and at the Ecole des Beaux Arts in 1864—and became a pupil of Edouard Frère during 1866–67. His paintings and watercolors were often exhibited at the Boston Athenaeum, the National Academy of Design, and the Paris Salon. Bacon visited Cairo and became noted for his use of Egyptian subject matter; he died there on March 13, 1912.

James Henry Beard was born in Buffalo, New York, on May 20, 1812 (other dates given: 1814 and 1815). In 1823 his family moved to Painesville, Ohio. At sixteen he took a few drawing lessons from an itinerant portrait painter named Hanks and studied briefly with Reuben Hitchcock. The following year he began traveling as an itinerant portraitist, first to Pittsburgh and subsequently to Cincinnati, Louisville, New Orleans, and other cities in the Southeast. About 1830 he settled in Cincinnati, having

completed his studies in painting. In the 1840's much notice was given to his genre pictures; in 1846 his *North Carolina Emigrants* sold for $750, said to have been the largest sum paid for a genre picture until that time. Beard's portrait compositions were often imitated and his depictions of animals were admired by many. Beard visited New York City in 1846–47 and from 1863–65, and settled there permanently in 1870. Two years later he was elected a member of the National Academy of Design. In spite of his age, Beard traveled daily from his home in Flushing, Long Island, to his studio on 34th Street and Broadway in Manhattan. He died in 1893, at the age of 81.

William Holbrook Beard was born in Painesville, Ohio, on April 13, 1824. He toured Ohio as an itinerant portrait painter and, in 1845, briefly joined his brother James Henry, an established genre painter, in New York City. Continuously on the move until about 1850, he finally settled in Buffalo, where he became a vital member of that city's growing art colony. In 1850 he sailed to Europe, where he studied in Rome and Düsseldorf for two years. Beard returned to Buffalo but moved permanently to New York City in 1860. He was elected a member of the National Academy of Design in 1863. Beard was popular for his genre scenes and pictures of anthropomorphized animals. When these lost their appeal, he returned to painting portraits for a living. He died in New York on February 20, 1900.

George Bellows was born in Columbus, Ohio, on August 12, 1882, and attended Ohio State University from 1901–04. He then moved to New York to study at the Art Students League and with Robert Henri at the New York School of Art. By 1906 Bellows was supporting himself as a newspaper illustrator and had rented a studio. His first exhibition in 1908 reveals the early and consistent influence of the technique and subject matter of Henri and The Eight. Bellows actively participated in the New York art world, as a teacher at the Art Students League, and by exhibiting and helping to organize such shows as the 1913 Armory Show. In 1918 he was elected an Academician at the National Academy of Design. The Metropolitan Museum of Art held a memorial exhibition of his work following his death in New York on January 8, 1925.

Frank Weston Benson, born March 24, 1862, in Salem, Massachusetts, was a dominant figure of the Boston art world at the turn of the century. From 1889 to 1917 he taught at the Boston Museum School, where he had studied from 1880–83. His education also included studies in Paris at the Académie Julian under Gustave Boulanger and Jules Lefebvre and a personal investigation of French plein-air painting. Benson, noted for his portrayals of women set in elegant surroundings, was recognized with a medal at the World's Columbian Exposition, Chicago, 1893; a Silver Medal at the Exposition Universelle, Paris, 1900; and a Gold Medal at the Louisiana Purchase Exposition, 1904. A retrospective exhibition of his work was held at the Corcoran Gallery of Art in 1920–21. Benson died in Salem on November 14, 1951.

George Caleb Bingham was born on March 20, 1811, on a farm west of Charlottesville, Virginia. In 1818 his family moved to Franklin, Missouri, a growing frontier town. At sixteen Bingham was apprenticed to a cabinetmaker, but his attention turned to painting. Largely self-taught, Bingham was painting portraits in Missouri and Mississippi by 1833. In 1838 he studied briefly at the Pennsylvania Academy of the Fine Arts and in 1840 exhibited six paintings at the National Academy of Design. From 1841–44 he kept a studio in the basement of the Capitol in Washington, D. C., where he painted portraits. He returned to Missouri in 1845 and there began to paint genre pictures, many of which were bought by the American Art-Union and popularized through engravings it distributed. He was also active in Whig politics and served in the Missouri State Legislature. From 1856–59 Bingham studied in Düsseldorf, Germany, and in 1859 he returned permanently to a life of painting and politics in Missouri. He died in Kansas City on July 7, 1879.

Charles F. Blauvelt was born in New York City in 1824. He studied drawing at the National Academy of Design, later became a pupil of Charles L. Elliott, and in 1847 began working as a portrait and genre painter, contributing frequently to gallery exhibitions in the East. Blauvelt was elected Academician at the National Academy of Design in 1859. He moved to Philadelphia in 1862, exhibiting at the Pennsylvania Academy of the Fine Arts where he became a member within three years. In 1867 he returned to New York and settled in Yonkers in 1869. Blauvelt later became Associate Professor of Drawing at the U. S. Naval Academy at Annapolis. He died in Greenwich, Connecticut, on April 16, 1900.

David Gilmour Blythe was born near East Liverpool, Ohio, on May 9, 1815. At sixteen he arrived in Pittsburgh and became apprenticed to Joseph Woodwell, working as a house painter and making decorative wood carvings. From 1837–40 he was in the Navy, traveling to New York, Boston, and the West Indies. He returned to Pittsburgh and began his artistic career as an itinerant portrait painter. He found his initial success in Uniontown, Pennsylvania, where he settled from 1846–51. There he met Julia Kaffer, whose death, less than a year after their mar-

riage in 1848, is often considered a cause of his aberrant artistic style. From 1850–51 Blythe assisted in the painting of a panoramic scene which toured Pennsylvania and Ohio with only moderate success. An itinerant painter for the next five years, Blythe returned to Pittsburgh in 1856. In the years following he produced what are now considered the best works of his career—genre scenes which reflected his satirical temperament. These pictures were often exhibited in the Wood Street art store of his patron, J. J. Gillespie. Blythe died an indigent on May 15, 1865.

Albertus (Alburtis) Del Orient Browere was born in Tarrytown, New York, on March 17, 1814. His father, John Henri Isaac Browere, was a sculptor and taker of life masks, but Albertus found his success in painting. At seventeen he exhibited at the National Academy of Design, and by 1833 he was painting portraits and illustrating the stories of Washington Irving. In 1841 his *Canonicus and the Governor of Plymouth* was acclaimed at the National Academy of Design. Living in the Catskills, Browere joined the artists of the Hudson River School in painting landscapes. He sailed twice to California: first in 1852, where he remained for four years, and again from 1858–61. In 1861 he returned to the Catskills permanently. Most of Browere's life was spent in financial hardship, and during his last years he made his living as a sign and wagon painter. He died in relative obscurity at Catskill, New York, February 17, 1887.

John George Brown was born in England on November 11, 1831. As a youth he was apprenticed for seven years to a glasscutter in Newcastle-on-Tyne, during which time he studied art with Scott Lauder, and later in Scotland with William B. Scott. By the age of twenty-two he was painting portraits in London, and within two years he was working in Brooklyn and studying under Thomas Cummings. Brown had his own studio by 1860 and began to paint children in rural settings. In 1869 Brown was elected President of the National Academy of Design. His sentimentalized city urchins, which he began painting in the 1870s, appealed to the public, and many were reproduced as prints. His studio at 51 West 10th Street was considered one of New York's art centers, and he was so successful that, by the end of his life, he was earning forty to fifty thousand dollars annually. He died in New York City on February 8, 1913.

Otis A. Bullard was born in Howard, New York, on February 25, 1816. At fourteen he was apprenticed to a sign and wagon painter. Inspired by an itinerant portrait painter, he left home in 1837 to study in Hartford, Connecticut, with the portrait artist Philip Hewins. In 1840 he began his own career as a portraitist in Amherst, Massa-

chusetts, and within three years he painted some nine hundred portraits (the whereabouts of only eight are known today). By 1843 Bullard had settled in New York City and was painting genre and historical pictures. He exhibited at the National Academy of Design from 1842–53 and at the American Art-Union in 1847–48. Bullard's most ambitious undertaking was a panorama of New York City, painted with several assistants between 1846–50. Financed by George Doel, the panorama traveled throughout the country and was last recorded in Detroit in May, 1867. Bullard died on October 13, 1853, in New York City, too early to realize the full success of his panorama.

William Henry Burr was a portrait and genre painter whose birth and death dates are not known. However, he exhibited at the National Academy of Design from 1841–59. He is mentioned in the New York City Directory of 1844 and of 1856, and is known to have briefly resided in Syracuse, New York, about 1846. He also exhibited at the Pennsylvania Academy of the Fine Arts in 1847 and at the American Art-Union in 1848.

John Carlin was born in Philadelphia on June 15, 1813. A deaf-mute, Carlin attended the Pennsylvania Institute for the Deaf and Dumb from 1821–25. He received drawing instruction at John R. Smith's academy, and studied portraits and genre pictures at the Artist's Fund Society in Philadelphia from 1835–38. He spent several years in Europe, studying antique sculpture at the British Museum and with Paul Delaroche in Paris. Carlin settled permanently in New York City in 1841. His popular works were exhibited frequently throughout the Northeast. He is also known for his novel, *The Scratchside Family* (c. 1861), and the poem "The Mute's Lament." Carlin was continually involved with the education of those mutually handicapped and was awarded an Honorary Master of Arts degree by the Columbia Institution for the Instruction of the Deaf, Dumb and Blind in 1864. He died in New York on April 23, 1891.

William Tolman Carlton was born in 1816. A portrait and genre painter, he is known to have exhibited at the Boston Athenaeum in 1836, 1842, and 1855, although he does not appear in the Boston directories until 1850. Records indicate that Carlton also exhibited a genre picture at the American Art-Union in New York in 1850. Little else is known of his life and career. He died in 1888.

Mary Cassatt was born May 22, 1844, in Allegheny City, Pennsylvania, and lived in Paris with her family from 1851–58. Studying formally from 1861–65 at the Pennsylvania Academy of the Fine Arts, she then supplemented

her education with extensive traveling through the European galleries, and in 1872 she exhibited at the Paris Salon. When her contribution to the 1877 Salon was refused, she joined Degas and the Impressionists, exhibiting with them in 1879, 1880, 1881, and 1886. While Cassatt lived and worked abroad, she was instrumental in the formation of the Havermeyer Collection now at the Metropolitan Museum of Art, New York. She had one-woman shows here and abroad from the 1890s on. Among her most important honors is the Gold Medal of Honor awarded her by the Pennsylvania Academy in 1914. Cassatt died at Château de Beaufresne, France, on June 14, 1926.

John Gadsby Chapman was born in Alexandria, Virginia, on December 8, 1808. After studying with George Cooke and Charles Bird King, he began his career as a painter-teacher in 1827, working in Winchester, Washington, and New York. He spent a year in Europe, chiefly in Rome and Florence. On his return in 1831, Chapman produced etchings and engravings for several New York publishing houses. A highly esteemed portraitist and historical painter, he was elected a Member of the National Academy of Design in 1836 and was instrumental in founding the Apollo Association and the Century Club. Chapman's most celebrated painting, *The Baptism of Pocahontas* (1840), hangs in the rotunda in the Capitol in Washington. In 1847 his manual *The American Drawing-Book* was published with great success. Chapman returned to Europe in 1848 and remained there until 1884. He died in Brooklyn, New York, on November 28, 1889.

William Merritt Chase was born November 1, 1849, in Nineveh, Indiana. Intermittently between 1867 and 1869 he studied with a local portrait painter, Benjamin Hayes. In 1869 Chase entered the National Academy of Design in New York and probably studied under J. O. Eaton. Chase's stay in Munich from 1872–78, with a nine-month visit to Venice in 1877, marked his artistic maturity. He studied in Munich with Alexander Wagner and Karl von Piloty, but the strongest influences were Wilhelm Leibl and Frank Duveneck. Returning to New York he began his long career as an influential artist, teacher, and tastemaker. Throughout his life Chase assimilated a succession of influences, including seventeenth-century Spanish and Dutch masters, Whistler, and the Impressionists. These in turn were transmitted to his followers. Among Chase's significant accomplishments were his establishment of the first plein-air painting school at Shinnecock, New York (1891–1902), his election to the Academy of Arts and Letters in 1908, and his numerous exhibitions here and abroad. Chase died in Atlantic City, New Jersey, on October 26, 1916.

William Worcester Churchill was born in 1858 in Jamaica Plains, Massachusetts. After studying in Paris under Léon Bonnat, Churchill settled in Boston. In 1911, he participated in the Boston Artists Exhibition at the Museum of Fine Arts. He also exhibited in the 1912 Annual at the Pennsylvania Academy of the Fine Arts. Churchill died in 1926 in Washington, D. C.

James Goodwyn Clonney was born on January 28, 1812, in Liverpool, England. As a young man he emigrated to the United States, and was working as a lithographic draftsman in New York City in 1830. He attended the antique school of the National Academy of Design, establishing himself as a miniaturist by 1834. In 1840 he became a naturalized citizen and within a year began to devote his time exclusively to genre painting. Clonney lived in New Rochelle, New York, from 1842–52; then he settled permanently in Cooperstown. His pictures were frequently exhibited at the National Academy of Design, the Apollo Association, and the American Art-Union. Clonney died in relative obscurity on October 7, 1867, in Binghamton, New York, where the local obituary referred to him as a farmer.

Eyre Crowe was born in Chelsea, London, on October 3, 1824. He grew up among artists and literary men, as his father was the writer Eyre Evans Crowe. As a youth he went to Paris to study under Paul Delaroche, with whom he went to Rome in 1843. Crowe returned to London in 1844 and later became a secretary and lifetime friend to William Makepeace Thackeray, whom he accompanied to the United States during 1852–53. Crowe wrote and illustrated a book on their travels entitled *With Thackeray in America* (published in 1893). In 1867 he was elected an Associate Member of the Royal Academy where he exhibited throughout his career. Crowe died in London on December 12, 1910.

Joseph Rodefer De Camp was born in Cincinnati, Ohio, November 5, 1858. He studied with Duveneck in Cincinnati and at the Munich Academy where John Alexander, John Twachtman, and William Merritt Chase were also students. He traveled to Florence and Venice in 1878 before returning to the United States in 1880. De Camp then set up a studio in Boston, and taught at the Boston Museum School and the Massachusetts Normal Art School. He was a member of and exhibited annually with the Ten American Painters and the Guild of Boston Artists. De Camp was known for his interior figure studies and portraits; his honors include the Temple Medal, Pennsylvania Academy of the Fine Arts, 1899; Honorable Mention, Paris Exposition, 1900; and the Gold Medal, St. Louis Exhibition, 1904. De Camp died in Medford, Massachusetts in 1923.

Asher Brown Durand was born in Maplewood (Jefferson Village), New Jersey, on August 21, 1796. He first learned engraving from his father who was a watchmaker and silversmith. From 1812–17 he was apprenticed to the noted engraver Peter Maverick, and his success at engraving Trumbull's *Declaration of Independence* (1820–23) established his reputation. Durand engraved portraits, landscapes, and banknotes until about 1835 when he took up painting. Durand was a founder of the Hudson River School, and sketched along the Hudson River, in the Adirondacks, and in the White Mountains. Financed by Jonathan Sturges, he traveled abroad in 1840 accompanied by the artists John F. Kensett, Thomas Rossiter, and John Casilear. In 1855 Durand published his thoughts on landscape painting in *The Crayon.* He was a founder of the National Academy of Design. He served as its president from 1845–61, and exhibited there annually from 1826 to the early 1870s. In poor health, he left New York permanently in 1869 and died in New Jersey on September 17, 1886.

George Henry Durrie was born in New Haven, Connecticut, on June 6, 1820. From 1839–40 he and his older brother John became students of the noted portrait painter Nathaniel Jocelyn. While still a student, George traveled through parts of Connecticut and New Jersey painting portraits. In 1843 he permanently settled in New Haven. His portraits were exhibited at the National Academy of Design and at the New Haven Horticultural Society; in 1845 he showed his first snow scene, and through the 1850s he occasionally exhibited landscapes and genre scenes. Durrie opened a studio in 1854 and held a public sale of his winter scenes. He visited New York City in 1857, possibly then contacting the lithographer Nathaniel Currier. Currier and Ives later reproduced many of his winter scenes and rural landscapes. He died on October 15, 1863, in New Haven.

Thomas Eakins was born July 25, 1844, in Philadelphia. In high school Eakins was interested in science and mathematics, mechanical drawing, and perspective. In 1861 Eakins enrolled at the Pennsylvania Academy of the Fine Arts where he drew from antique casts. Simultaneously, he studied anatomy at Jefferson Medical School, actually dissecting cadavers and watching operations. His stay in Paris, 1866–69, whe e he studied with Jean Léon Gérôme and Léon Bonnat, and a trip to Spain, 1869, where he saw   rks of Diego Velázquez and José de Ribera, led him   n and develop his realistic style. He re-   phia in 1869. When in 1876 he became   n instr   d in 1882 director of the Pennsylvania Academy of the Fine Arts, he encouraged his students to study anatomy and to paint directly from a living model. His art teaching methods were often met with hostility and he was forced to resign his directorship in 1886. He also experimented with photography and motion-picture studies. In 1902 he was elected to the National Academy of Design. His health began to fail after 1910 and he died on June 25, 1916, in his home in Philadelphia.

Francis William Edmonds was born in Hudson, New York, on November 22, 1806. As a youth his only training was copying engravings. In 1823 he was sent to New York to work as a clerk at the Tradesmen's Bank. Three years later he studied at the National Academy of Design. In the late 1820s Edmonds worked for engravers of bank notes, and in 1829 he first exhibited at the National Academy of Design. From 1836–38 he exhibited under the pseudonym E. F. Williams. In 1830 Edmonds was appointed to the Hudson River Bank in Hudson, New York, but returned to New York City within two years. He was accepted into the National Academy of Design in 1837, and in 1840 became treasurer for the Apollo Association, later the American Art-Union. He left for Europe in November, 1840, meeting with friends such as Asher Brown Durand and John F. Kensett; he returned within nine months. Throughout his life Edmonds was an active businessman, politician, and banker as well as an artist. He spent the last years of his life at "Crow's Nest," his thirty-room stone mansion on the Bronx River, New York, where he died on February 7, 1863.

John Whetten Ehninger was born in New York City on July 22, 1827. He graduated from Columbia College in 1847, then spent the next six years in Europe, studying with Emanuel Leutze in Düsseldorf and in Paris with Thomas Couture. On his return he settled in New York City, devoting his time to genre subjects which were frequently exhibited. Ehninger was elected a Member of the National Academy of Design in 1860. He frequently traveled abroad, and while in Europe made designs for the *London Illustrated Times* and the *London Illustrated News.* He also illustrated a gift edition of Longfellow's *Courtship of Miles Standish.* Ehninger died of apoplexy at Saratoga Springs, New York, on January 22, 1889.

Alvan T. Fisher was born August 9, 1792, in Needham, Massachusetts. He grew up in Dedham, where he worked as a shoe clerk and an accountant. Against his family's wishes, Fisher taught himself the rudiments of painting and studied with John Ritto Penniman, an ornamental painter. At twenty-one Fisher was painting cheap portraits; by 1815 he was producing landscapes and animal and genre pictures, which sold well at the auctions he organized. The first ten years of Fisher's career were occupied by commissions that required extensive travel. In 1825 he went to Europe, studying chiefly in Paris. He

returned to Boston within a year, where he was allegedly the first landscape painter to advertise his specialty. His records reveal that after 1826 he sold some 800 paintings, mostly landscapes and portraits. An Honorary Member of the National Academy of Design, his works were also exhibited at the Boston Athenaeum nearly every year from 1827 until his death on February 13, 1863.

Edwin Forbes was born in New York City in 1839. His formal art training began in 1857 and within two years he became a pupil of Arthur F. Tait. When the Civil War broke out Forbes joined the Potomac Army, working as an artist for *Frank Leslie's Illustrated Newspaper* from 1862–64. Returning to New York in 1865, he used his battle scene sketches as studies for paintings. A series of copperplate etchings, "Life Studies of the Great Army," were exhibited in Philadelphia in 1877 and earned him a medal as well as Honorary Membership to the London Etching Club. Some time in 1878 Forbes set up his studio in Brooklyn, painting genre, landscape, and animal pictures. He frequently exhibited at the National Academy of Design and at the Boston Athenaeum. Forbes died in Brooklyn on March 6, 1895.

William J. Glackens was born March 13, 1870, in Philadelphia. Like other members of the Ashcan School (The Eight), Glackens worked as an artist-reporter from 1891–95 while attending night classes at the Pennsylvania Academy of the Fine Arts. He and Robert Henri shared a studio in 1894 and traveled to Holland and Paris to study the Dutch and Fontainebleau masters in 1895. Despite his dislike for illustrating, Glackens continued to do so as a means of support until 1914. Though Glackens's own works were exhibited irregularly, he frequently organized group exhibitions which included other artists rejected by the American academic painting establishment. The Whitney Museum held a memorial exhibition, directed by his friends, following his death in New York on May 22, 1938.

Francis Guy was born in Lorton, near Keswick, in the English Lake District, in 1760. He worked in London as a silk dyer until December, 1795, when he emigrated to New York. After several unsuccessful attempts to set up dye works in Brooklyn and Philadelphia, he left for Baltimore in 1798. He advertised as a landscapist and historical painter, devoting himself exclusively to painting, and met financial success by selling his works at public raffles and auctions. Among his important commissions were a view of the Baltimore Cathedral and several marine battle scenes painted during the War of 1812. Guy wrote an autobiography which he was never able to publish. In 1817 he returned to New York, where he died on August 12, 1820.

Seymour Joseph Guy was born in Greenwich, England, on January 16, 1824. He began to study painting at the age of fifteen with the marine painter Thomas Buttersworth. He also studied at the Royal Academy and the British Museum, and in 1843 he became apprenticed to Ambrose Jerome under whom he refined his portrait techniques. Guy emigrated to the United States in 1854, settling in New York City. His talents as a portraitist were quickly recognized and his genre scenes of children were very popular. Guy was elected an Academician of the National Academy of Design in 1865, and his works were also exhibited in Boston and Maryland. He died in New York on December 10, 1910, after a long career.

William Hahn was born Karl Wilhelm Hahn in Ebersbach, Saxony, Germany, on January 7, 1829. At fourteen he entered the Royal Academy of Art in Dresden and studied with Julius Hübner. He emigrated to the United States some time around 1870, and had a studio in Boston by late 1871. In 1872 he moved to San Francisco, and exhibited regularly at the newly formed San Francisco Art Association from 1872–77 and periodically until 1883. From 1878 to 1881 he exhibited annually at the National Academy of Design, using a New York City address. Hahn was a popular and productive genre painter who found patrons in two of the most influential families of California: the Crockers and the Stanfords. His canvases are historical documents of California life and landscape. A member of the Bohemian Club and the Graphic Club of San Francisco, he worked among such artists as William Keith, Charles Nahl, and William Coulter. Hahn returned to Europe some time in 1883 and died in Dresden in 1887.

Lilian Westcott Hale was born on January 7, 1881, in Hartford, Connecticut. A pupil of Edmund Tarbell and William Merritt Chase, Hale also studied at the Connecticut Academy of Fine Arts and the Concord Artists' Academy. Her awards include the Gold Medal and Medal of Honor from the Panama-Pacific Exposition, San Francisco, 1915, and the Gold Medal from the Philadelphia Art Club, 1919. She died in Dedham, Massachusetts, in 1963.

Frederick Childe Hassam was born in Boston on October 17, 1859. Better known as Childe Hassam, he received his first art instruction in the graphic arts, earning his living as a freelance illustrator and lithographer. From 1878–83 Hassam attended Boston Art Club evening classes, the Lowell Institute, and classes with I. M. Gaugengigi, a Boston painter. His first exhibition, in Boston, 1883, was of watercolors, since Hassam did not begin to paint full time until 1886 during his second European work-study trip. In Paris, Hassam studied at the Académie Julian

under the leading academicians Gustave Boulanger and Jules Lefebvre, and exhibited in the Salon in 1887 and 1888. His real influences were, however, the Barbizon and Impressionist groups and later, Whistler. Settling in New York in 1889, Hassam became an influential part of the establishment. He was an original member of the Ten American Painters and began his own school at Essex. His moderate version of Impressionism was well received, earning him awards like the one at the World's Columbian Exhibition, 1893, and election to the National Academy of Design, 1906. Aside from his annual exhibitions, Hassam also showed at the Armory in 1913. Hassam died in Easthampton, New York, on August 27, 1935.

Robert Henri was born in Cincinnati, Ohio, on June 25, 1865. He studied at the Pennsylvania Academy of the Fine Arts under Thomas Anshutz from 1886–88, subsequently attending the Académie Julian and the Ecole des Beaux Arts in Paris until 1891. Henri combined independent study and travel in repeated trips to Europe throughout his life. Settling in New York, he became established as a teacher and as a painter of street scenes. His first one-man show was held at the Macbeth Galleries, New York, in 1902. Henri also participated in the 1908 exhibition of The Eight at Macbeth, the 1910 Society of Independent Artists Exhibition, and the 1913 Armory Show. Henri was a recipient of many significant awards, and remained active as a teacher until his death in New York on July 12, 1929.

Edward Lamson Henry was born in Charleston, South Carolina, on January 12, 1841. He grew up in New York City, receiving his first artistic training from Walter M. Oddie in 1855. For two years he was a student at the Pennsylvania Academy of the Fine Arts and in 1860 he sailed to Europe. Henry traveled the grand tour and studied briefly under Charles Gleyre and Gustave Courbet in Paris. Returning in 1862, he settled in New York, where his American and European genre pictures soon became popular. In the fall of 1864, Henry served in the Union Army, and made sketches which he later used for his Civil War paintings. Henry's hobby was photography. In 1869 he was elected a Member of the National Academy of Design. His pictures were often reproduced and he kept a studio in the famous Tenth Street Studio Building, until 1885. Revisiting Europe in 1871, 1875, and, for the last time, 1881, he finally settled in Crogsmoor, New York, in 1887. He died in Ellenville, New York, on May 11, 1919.

Thomas Hicks was born on October 18, 1823, in Newtown, Pennsylvania. His relative, the Quaker artist Edward Hicks, was his first painting teacher. Hicks also studied at the Pennsylvania Academy of the Fine Arts and, from 1845–49, in Europe, specifically in Paris, under Thomas Couture, and by drawing from antique casts. Settling in New York in 1849, Hicks began his successful career as a portrait painter. He portrayed such famous Americans as Henry Ward Beecher, Henry Wadsworth Longfellow, Harriet Beecher Stowe, and Abraham Lincoln. In 1851 the National Academy elected Hicks a Member. He died in Trenton Falls, New York, October 8, 1890.

Winslow Homer was born in Boston on February 24, 1836. He grew up in Cambridge and at the age of nineteen was apprenticed to the Boston lithographer, J. H. Bufford. He regularly illustrated for *Harper's Weekly* and *Ballou's Pictorial* from 1857–59 at which time he moved to New York City, there to continue on a freelance basis until 1875. Homer attended night classes at the National Academy of Design in 1861 and drawing classes in Brooklyn, receiving occasional painting instruction from Frédéric Rondel. In 1865 he was elected a Member of the National Academy of Design. Crucial to Homer's development as a realist were his activities as artist-correspondent for *Harper's* during the Civil War. He went to Paris in 1867 and to Tynemouth, England, in 1881. In 1884 he settled permanently in a cottage built on a cliff, overlooking the ocean at Prout's Neck, Maine. He made several trips to Quebec and the Adirondacks in the summers and to Florida and the Bahamas in the winters, which inspired many watercolors as well as oils. Homer's reputation and popularity grew continuously and he received numerous awards for his accomplishments. After a long illness he died at Prout's Neck on September 29, 1910.

Thomas Hovenden was born on December 28, 1840, in Cork, Ireland. He studied at the Cork School of Design and at the age of twenty-three he moved to New York. Financially unable to pursue an artist's career, he made a living as a frame maker while attending night classes at the National Academy of Design. In 1874 Hovenden went to Paris, finally devoting his full attention to painting. He studied at the Ecole des Beaux Arts with Alexandre Cabanel and in Pont-Aven, Brittany, exhibiting at the Salon of 1876 and at the International Exhibition of 1878. Returning to the United States in 1880, he married artist Helen Carson and settled at Plymouth Meeting, Pennsylvania. They shared her studio, in a house used by the Carsons as a center for the Underground Railroad and abolitionists' meetings during the Civil War. From this association stems Hovenden's interest in the war and the portrayal of its black heroes. Hovenden taught at the Pennsylvania Academy of the Fine Arts; Robert Henri was among his students. At the 1893 World's Columbian Exposition in Chicago, he reached his peak of popularity with his *Breaking Home Ties*. He was also known for his plein-air landscapes. Hovenden was killed by a train near Trenton, New Jersey, on August 14, 1895.

Henry Inman was born in Utica, New York, on October 28, 1801. In 1812 his family moved to New York City, where he attended drawing school. In 1814 he became apprenticed to John Wesley Jarvis. The apprenticeship lasted seven years, but the friendship between student and master continued long after. In 1821 Inman set up his own studio, painting portraits and some miniatures. He participated in establishing the National Academy of Design in 1826 and was its vice president, 1826–31, 1839–42, and 1844. From 1826–28 he worked in partnership with his pupil, Thomas S. Cummings. In 1831 Inman moved to Philadelphia, where he became a partner in the lithographic firm of Childs & Inman, and Director of the Pennsylvania Academy of the Fine Arts. In 1834 he returned permanently to New York. Inman was afflicted with asthma, and as his health steadily declined, so did his artistic production. In 1844 he visited England for about a year and exhibited at the Royal Academy. After a month of critical illness, Inman died in New York on January 17, 1846.

Eastman Johnson was born in Lovell, Maine, on July 29, 1824. He began his career by drawing crayon portraits of his neighbors in Augusta, Maine. In 1844–45 he moved to Washington, D. C. and established a successful practice drawing government officials. In 1846 Henry Wadsworth Longfellow persuaded him to move to Cambridge, Massachusetts. In 1849 he went to Europe, studying in Düsseldorf, at The Hague (where he earned his living painting portraits), and in Paris. He returned to Washington, D. C. in 1855, and in 1856–57 he made two trips to Superior, Wisconsin. He moved permanently to New York City in 1858. His fame came when he exhibited *Negro Life in the South* in 1859 at the National Academy of Design, where he became an Associate in 1859 and a full Academician in 1860. During the 1860s, the Civil War and the maplesugar camps were sources for his subject matter. He summered on Nantucket beginning in the 1870s, where his paintings of cranberry pickers are among his best. From the mid-1880s on, he mainly painted commissioned portraits. He died in New York City on April 5, 1906.

David Claypool Johnston was born in Philadelphia on March 25, 1798 (1797 and 1799 have also been given). He became an apprentice to the engraver Francis Kearney in 1815, and by 1819 had his own business. Unsuccessful as an engraver, Johnston turned to acting and joined the New Theater in Philadelphia. However, he continued to engrave theatrical portraits and caricatures, and he ended his stage career in Boston in 1825, when he found a responsive audience for his graphic talents. Working for Pendelton's lithograph house, Johnston was one of the pioneers of lithography in the United States. In 1828 he began publishing "Scraps," an annual folio containing humorous illustrations of political and social life. He was dubbed "the American Cruikshank" for modeling his an-

nual after the English artist's "Scraps and Sketches." Throughout his life he painted comical genre scenes; of these, many watercolors but few oils are known. In his later years he taught painting and mechanical drawing. Johnston died in Dorchester, Massachusetts, on November 8, 1865.

Theodor Kaufmann was born on December 18, 1814, in Hanover, Germany. He studied painting under Peter Von Cornelius in Düsseldorf and with Wilhelm Von Kaulbach in Munich; his chief involvement was with religious subjects. Joining the Revolution, he fought on the barricades in Dresden, but in 1850 fled from the suppression of the Prussian Army, first to Switzerland, and then to Belgium. He finally emigrated to the United States that year, and opened a studio in New York. He set up a drawing school which was attended by one student—Thomas Nast, the future political cartoonist. Following the failure of his school, he earned a living painting portraits and assisting in a photographic studio. Kaufmann traveled along the East Coast and in 1860, at the age of forty-six, enlisted for active service in the Civil War. After the war he continued to support the Union cause as a speaker and writer in St. Louis, and then settling in Boston, he produced paintings of the Civil War that won great popularity. In 1869 his paintings were exhibited in Munich and Vienna, and in 1871 he published *The American Painting Book*. In his last years Kaufmann was lost from public sight. He died in New York in 1900.

Charles Bird King was born in Newport, Rhode Island, in 1785. He first studied painting with Edward Savage. In 1805 he went to London where he studied with Benjamin West and met Thomas Sully. During his time in Europe he became familiar with artistic traditions such as *trompe l'oeil* and *vanitas,* which he employed in his own still lifes. In 1812 he went to Philadelphia; later he moved to Washington, D.C., where he received numerous commissions. Although King was personally liked by his contemporaries, his art did not generate much enthusiasm. In the early 1820s he painted the portraits of some famous North American Indian chiefs and their wives who were visiting Washington. These remained in the artist's personal collection until his death on March 18, 1862, when they became part of the collection at the Smithsonian Institution; however, the majority were burned in the 1865 fire at the Smithsonian.

Robert Koehler, born December 27, 1850, in Hamburg, Germany, was both a printmaker and a painter. His family moved to Milwaukee in 1854, and he was apprenticed to a lithographer in 1866. In 1871 he moved to Pittsburgh and then to New York, where he attended night classes at the National Academy of Design. From 1873–75 he studied in Munich under Ludwig von Löfftz. He re-

turned to New York, 1875–79, where he first exhibited at the National Academy of Design in 1877, but was back in Munich from 1879–92. There he organized the American section of art exhibitions held in 1883 and 1888. He returned to the United States and was Director of the Minneapolis School of Fine Arts from 1893–1917. He belonged to the Minneapolis Art League, the Minneapolis Society of Western Artists, and the State Art Society. Koehler died on April 4, 1917, in Milwaukee, Wisconsin.

John Lewis Krimmel was born in 1789 in Württemberg, Germany, where he received art training from Johann Baptist Seele, a painter of military subjects. In 1810 he emigrated to the United States accompanied by Alexander Rider, a miniaturist. Krimmel joined his brother in Philadelphia and was given a position in his counting house, a post Krimmel soon gave up for a painting career. In 1817 he returned to Germany, but was back in Philadelphia within two years. Influenced by David Wilkie, Krimmel painted genre scenes which were exhibited annually in Philadelphia; his contemporaries called him "the American Hogarth." In 1821 Krimmel was elected President of the Association of American Artists. Shortly thereafter, he accidentally drowned in a millpond near Germantown, Pennsylvania, on July 15, 1821.

George Cochran Lambdin was born in Pittsburgh, Pennsylvania, in 1830. At the age of eight he was taken to Philadelphia where he remained, with the exception of a few years spent in traveling, for most of his life. He studied painting with his father, James Reid Lambdin, a well-known portrait painter, and by 1848 he was exhibiting at the Pennsylvania Academy of the Fine Arts. Lambdin went to Europe to tour the Continent from 1855–57 and again in 1870. In 1858 he exhibited at the National Academy of Design in New York, and spent two years in that city; he was accepted as an Academician at the National Academy in 1868. Best known today for his genre pictures, Lambdin was quite successful as a portraitist as well as a painter of floral still lifes. He died in Philadelphia on January 28, 1896.

William Henry Lippincott was born in 1849 in Philadelphia. First studying at the Pennsylvania Academy of the Fine Arts, he became known as an illustrator and later a scenic designer. Lippincott entered Léon Bonnat's Paris studio in 1874 and remained in France for eight years, regularly exhibiting at Paris Salons. Upon his return in 1882 to New York, Lippincott contributed frequently to American art exhibitions, notably at the National Academy of Design and the Society of American Artists, and was known for his portraits and child-life scenes. In 1896, he was elected a Member of the National Academy, having previously taught there. Lippincott died in 1920 in New York.

George M. Luks was born in Williamsport, Pennsylvania, on August 13, 1867. He studied at the Pennsylvania Academy of the Fine Arts and at the Düsseldorf Academy; however, his strongest influences were from his independent study of seventeenth-century French and Spanish masters. Starting his career as a newspaper artist in Philadelphia, Luks covered the Spanish-American War in Cuba and later drew caricatures for the comics page. A vital, if not boisterous man, Luks was a member of The Eight, and a participant in the 1913 Armory Show. He was also a teacher at the Art Students League, and a member of the American Society of Sculptors and Engravers and the New York Water Color Club. Luks received such awards as the Temple Gold Medal, Pennsylvania Academy of the Fine Arts, 1916; the Logan Medal, Art Institute of Chicago, 1926; and the first William A. Clark Prize and the Corcoran Gold Medal, Corcoran Gallery of Art, 1932. Until his death in New York on October 29, 1933, Luks painted all aspects of urban life.

Tompkins Harrison Matteson was born in Peterboro, New York, on May 9, 1813. He went to school in Hamilton and traveled around New York State as an actor for several years. He moved to New York City in 1841 and studied at the National Academy of Design. Matteson opened a studio, painting portraits and genre scenes, but he made his reputation as an historical painter with such works as *The Spirit of '76*. In 1851 Matteson settled permanently in Sherburne, New York, where he participated in community affairs while continuing to paint. He died there on February 2, 1884.

Christian Mayr, born about 1805, was a native of Germany; his name first appeared in United States directories in 1834 as an exhibitor at the National Academy of Design in New York. Little is known about the life of this artist. In 1839 he went to Boston. His first recorded visit to Charleston, South Carolina, was in 1840; he maintained a studio there and revisited frequently until 1843. In Charleston he produced portraits, historical paintings, "fancy paintings," and genre scenes, as well as daguerreotypes. Mayr earned a substantial income by raffling his paintings and advertised these raffles regularly in the Charleston *Currier*. He visited New Orleans in 1844, returning to New York within a year, where he remained for the rest of his life. In 1836 he was made an Associate of the National Academy of Design and was elected an Academician in 1849. He died on October 19, 1851.

Thomas Moran was born in Bolton, England, on January 12, 1837. In 1844 his family emigrated to the United States. After his apprenticeship under a wood engraver in Philadelphia, he turned to painting, aided by his brother Edward. Moran visited England in 1862 where, in the London National Gallery, he was captivated by Turner's

landscapes. He copied many of these and remained under their influence throughout his life. In 1866–67 he made another European visit, this time traveling to France and Italy. In 1871, Moran joined a government expedition to Yellowstone Park. His watercolor sketches of these Western sights were published in 1876 as chromolithographs. Moran was elected a Member of the National Academy of Design in 1884 and he exhibited there frequently. He made visits to the West to paint the scenery, and in 1916 he moved to Santa Barbara, California, where he died on August 26, 1926.

William Sidney Mount was born on November 26, 1807, in Setauket, Long Island, and was raised in Stony Brook. At seventeen he was apprenticed to his brother Henry, a sign painter living in New York. He attended classes at the National Academy of Design in 1826 and was elected an Academician within four years. From 1829–36 he worked mostly in New York, but in 1837 he returned to Stony Brook. Though his primary means of support were his portraits, Mount is best known for his scenes of rural life. He exhibited frequently at the National Academy of Design through the 1830s, 1840s, and 1850s, but the works he produced in the last decade of his life were little seen. He died in Setauket on November 19, 1868.

Jerome Myers, who moved to New York City at nineteen, was born March 20, 1867, in Petersburg, Virginia. Myers first worked as a scene painter for New York theaters, studying at night at Cooper Union and later at the Art Students League. His characteristic themes of city life were first shown at Macbeth Gallery in 1908, and he also exhibited with The Eight. Participating regularly in group exhibitions, Myers was especially active in the organization of the 1913 Armory Show. Myers was the recipient of such honors as the Carnegie Prize, 1936, and the Isidor Prize, 1938. Before his death in New York on June 29, 1940, Myers published his autobiography *Artist in Manhattan.*

Johannes Adam Simon Oertel was born near Nuremberg, Germany, on November 3, 1823. From 1836–48, planning to enter the ministry, he studied with a Reverend Loche, while also training as an engraver and painter at the Polytechnic Institute at Nuremberg, and under J. M. Enzing-Müller in Munich. Oertel emigrated to the United States in 1848 and secured a teaching position in a women's seminary in Newark, New Jersey. In 1851 he was in Madison, New Jersey, painting religious subjects with little success; he then turned to engraving bank notes and painting portraits and animal pictures. In 1855 he moved to Brooklyn, New York, only to leave for Washington, D.C., in 1857 on a commission to paint mural decorations for the House of Representatives. In Wash-

ington until 1859, Oertel was occupied with minor designs instead of the promised murals. Always attempting to win some recognition for his religious paintings, Oertel exhibited them regularly in various cities. They did not, however, spark much enthusiasm outside religious communities. In 1871 he settled in Washington, D.C., as an Episcopal priest, painting altarpieces and panels for churches in many Southern states. Oertel spent the last years of his life in Vienna, Virginia, and died there on December 9, 1909.

William McGregor Paxton, born in Baltimore, May 6, 1869, was a pupil of Dennis Bunker in Boston and of Jean Léon Gérôme in Paris. From 1906–13 he taught at the Boston Museum School. Noted as a figure and portrait painter, Paxton was a member of the Guild of Boston Artists and was elected to the National Academy of Design in 1917. His work is represented in the Metropolitan Museum of Art, the Museum of Fine Arts, Boston, and the Corcoran Gallery of Art. Paxton died in Newton, Massachusetts, in 1941.

John Quidor was born in Tappan, New York, on January 26, 1801. His family moved to New York City when he was ten, and some time between 1813 and 1822 he was apprenticed to John Wesley Jarvis; this ended when Quidor's father sued Jarvis for improper instruction. From the forty-five years of Quidor's sporadic artistic activity, few works were recorded or are known today. In 1828 he exhibited for the first time at the National Academy of Design, and within the next decade he exhibited only twice more. Known during his lifetime primarily as a sign painter, Quidor is remembered today for his imaginative literary paintings. From 1843–49 he worked on a commission from a Methodist minister to paint seven huge biblical scenes in exchange for a farm in Illinois, which he never received. He went West some time between 1847 and 1851, settling near St. Louis. In 1868 Quidor moved to his daughter's home in Jersey City, where he died on December 13, 1881.

William Tylee Ranney was born in Middletown, Connecticut, on May 9, 1813. At thirteen he was taken to Fayetteville, North Carolina, where he was apprenticed to a tinsmith. In 1833 he was studying drawing in Brooklyn, but he joined the army during the Mexican War. He returned to New York and began to exhibit at the National Academy of Design, finally setting up his own portrait studio in 1843. Ranney settled permanently in Hoboken, New Jersey, in 1848, painting historical, Western, and genre pictures. In 1850 he was elected Associate Member of the National Academy of Design and exhibited there frequently almost until his death, from pulmonary tuberculosis, on November 8, 1857.

Platt Powell Ryder was born June 11, 1821 in Brooklyn, New York. In 1850 he began to exhibit his portraits and genre pictures at the National Academy of Design and was finally elected an Associate of the Academy in 1868. His first and only trip abroad was made as late as 1869–70, for study in Paris and London. Instrumental in establishing the Brooklyn Academy of Design, Ryder spent most of his life in the midst of the New York art world. He died in Saratoga Springs, New York, on July 17, 1896.

John Singer Sargent was born January 12, 1856, in Florence, Italy, of American parents. As a child, Sargent traveled extensively in Europe with his parents. His formal art education began in the studio of the German-American painter Carl Welsch, in Rome, 1868–69. Sargent also studied at the Academia delle Belle Arti in Florence, 1870, and in Carolus Duran's studio in Paris, 1874. Following his first visit to the United States in 1876, he made his first entry to the Paris Salon in 1877, and to the Society of American Artists in 1878. Throughout his life Sargent traveled and worked abroad, visiting places such as Morocco, Holland, Venice, and Egypt. Famous for his elegant and painterly portraiture, Sargent also received commissions to decorate the Boston Public Library, 1895–1912, the rotunda at the Boston Museum of Fine Arts, 1921, and the Harvard University Widener Library, 1922. A cosmopolitan artist, as was his friend and mentor Whistler, Sargent had his first one-man exhibition at the St. Botolph's Club, Boston, in 1888, and exhibited nine pictures at the Chicago World's Fair of 1893. Sargent died in London on April 15, 1925.

Hyppolite Victor Valentin Sebron was born in Caudelbec, France, on August 21, 1801. He lived in the United States from 1849–55. Chiefly occupied as a painter of dioramas and genre pictures, he worked in New Orleans from 1851–52 and was in New York City in 1854. Sebron died in Paris on September 1, 1897.

Everett Shinn was born in 1873, in Woodstown, New Jersey. Trained in industrial design and engineering, Shinn worked as a designer before studying at the Pennsylvania Academy of the Fine Arts under Thomas Anshutz. In 1889, two years after settling in New York, Shinn had his first one-man show at Boussod-Valadon Galleries, the same year he exhibited at the Pennsylvania Academy and at the St. Louis Exposition. Shinn exhibited with The Eight in the 1908 Macbeth Galleries show and in other group shows throughout his career. He illustrated books and stories and drew many cartoons. He also painted murals for the City Hall of Trenton, New Jersey. He enjoyed putting on short dramatic pieces, and in 1917 he went to work for Samuel Goldwyn at Goldwyn Pictures. He was later art director for other movie studios. A flamboyant

character who married four times, Shinn was allegedly the model for the bohemian artist depicted in Theodore Dreiser's *The Genius* (1911). Shinn died on May 1, 1953, in New York City.

John Sloan was born August 2, 1871, in Lock Haven, Pennsylvania. First recognized as an illustrator and advertiser, Sloan was included in several major exhibitions in 1900, and encouraged by Robert Henri to consider seriously a career as a painter and subsequently a teacher. Sloan taught himself etching, but learned drawing at the Spring Garden Institute as well as from Thomas Anshutz, and was a pupil of Thomas Eakins at the Pennsylvania Academy of the Fine Arts. Sloan participated in the exhibition of The Eight at the Macbeth Galleries in 1908 and exhibited with the Society of Independent Artists in 1910. For his time, Sloan's art and politics were considered radical, and he joined the Socialist Party, 1912–14, becoming acting art editor of *The Masses*. Beginning in 1915 Sloan received an increasing number of honors from the art establishment. Among his most important are the Bronze Medal at the Panama-Pacific International, 1915; the Metropolitan Museum of Art's acquisition of his work, 1921; election to the Academy of Arts and Letters, 1942; a retrospective exhibition at the Kraushaar Gallery, 1948; and a retrospective exhibition at the Whitney Museum of American Art, 1952. Sloan died after an operation on September 7, 1952, in Hanover, New Hampshire.

Lilly Martin Spencer was born in Exeter, England, on November 26, 1822 of French school-teachers. In 1830 the family sailed to the United States and settled in New York City, but they moved to Marietta, Ohio, in 1833, where she studied oil painting techniques with two local artists. Spencer's first exhibition was held in the summer of 1841; her father then took her to Cincinnati where she could receive instruction from James H. Beard. Spencer earned her living as a portraitist, and by 1846 she had become one of the most popular genre painters in Cincinnati. In 1849 she returned to New York City and was made an Honorary Member of the National Academy of Design. She settled in Newark, New Jersey, in 1858. The mother of thirteen children, seven of whom lived to adulthood, Spencer was actively painting until her last days. She died at Crum's Elbow, New York, on May 22, 1902.

Julius L. Stewart was born in Philadelphia on September 6, 1855. A pupil of Jean Léon Gérôme and Raimundo de Madrazo in Paris, Stewart's paintings demonstrate the elegance of the French school but remain true to the style prevailing among the American artists' colony in Paris. Though he chose Paris for his permanent residence, Stewart was an active member of numerous organizations both in Europe and the United States. He served on several

juries responsible for the selection of works exhibited and was an influential mediator on both sides of the Atlantic. In 1899 he was elected a member of the Societé National des Beaux-Arts having received, among other distinctions, the Godal Medal at the Berlin International Art Exhibition, 1891; Grand Gold Medal, Berlin, 1895, and Munich, 1897. Stewart died January 5, 1919, in Paris.

Arthur Fitzwilliam Tait was born in Liverpool, England, in August, 1819. He developed his interest in art when he worked at the House of Agnew and Ganette, an art store in Manchester, and taught himself to paint. In 1850 he emigrated to New York, where he set up his studio. Tait specialized in sporting scenes—popular with art dealers—and his pictures were exhibited annually at the National Academy of Design and reproduced by various lithography houses. In 1852 Tait met John Osborn, who became a generous patron. He spent many summers in the forests of the Adirondacks and other regions of northern New York studying and sketching wildlife. Tait was elected a Member of the National Academy of Design in 1858. He died at his home in Yonkers, New York, on April 28, 1905.

Henry Ossawa Tanner was born in Pittsburgh on June 21, 1859. His father was a Bishop of the African Methodist Episcopal Church, and Henry grew up in an educated black middle-class environment. He was enrolled in the Pennsylvania Academy of the Fine Arts in 1880 as a student of Thomas Eakins, who influenced his early style. Tanner taught at Clark College in Atlanta and with the help of his patrons, Bishop and Mrs. Joseph C. Hartzell, held an exhibition of his paintings in Cincinnati. Discouraged by the failure of his show, he left for France in 1891, where he resumed his studies at the Académie Julian. He was subsequently elected to the French Academy. Tanner rarely revisited the United States, though he won many awards on both sides of the Atlantic. Primarily successful for his biblical subjects, he remained unimpressed by modernism, spending his last years in relative isolation. He died in Paris on May 25, 1937.

Edmund Charles Tarbell, born April 26, 1862, in West Croton, Massachusetts, was an influential artist and teacher in the Boston area. Before studying along with Frank W. Benson and Robert Reid at the Boston Museum School during 1880–83, Tarbell apprenticed at Forbes Lithograph Co. (c. 1877–80). His mature work is also a result of his Parisian studies at the Académie Julian under Gustave Boulanger and Jules Lefebvre and his familiarity with French Impressionist innovations. Tarbell, with Frank W. Benson, Julian Alden Weir, Willard Metcalf, Joseph R. De Camp, Thomas Dewing, Edward Simmons, John Twachtman, Robert Reid, and Frederick Childe Hassam, founded Ten American Painters in 1898, simulating an academy of American Impressionism. Well established during his lifetime, Tarbell received such honors as an award at the World's Columbian Exposition, Chicago, 1893; a Bronze Medal at the Paris Exposition, 1900; and membership to the Panama-Pacific Exposition, San Francisco, 1915. Tarbell consistently painted genteel subjects in technically superior compositions, until his death on August 1, 1938, in New Castle, Massachusetts.

Jerome B. Thompson was born on January 30, 1814, in Middleboro, Massachusetts. The son of a well-known portrait painter, Cephas G. Thompson, he worked as a sign and ornament painter and, while still in his teens, moved to Cape Cod, where he set up his studio for painting portraits. In 1835 he went to New York City, exhibiting at the National Academy of Design; he was elected an Associate Member in 1851. The following year he went to England, studying there for years. Thompson painted landscapes and genre pictures of rustic life. He was admired by contemporaries for his devotion to American subjects, and his pictures became popularized through engravings. Thompson died in Glen Gardens, New Jersey, where he had lived in semiretirement for many years, on May 1, 1886.

Stacey Tolman was born January 28, 1860, in Concord, Massachusetts. Known primarily as a portrait painter, Tolman also depicted indoor scenes of middle-class life. His formal education here and abroad influenced his work throughout his career. He was a pupil of Otto Grundmann in Boston and of Gustave Boulanger, Jules Lefebvre, and Alexandre Cabanel in Paris. After settling in Providence, Rhode Island, Tolman died there in 1935.

Charles Frederick Ulrich, born October 18, 1858, in New York City, studied at the National Academy of Design, New York, and later with Ludwig von Löfftz and Wilhelm Lindenschmit in Munich. In 1884, Ulrich was honored as the first recipient of the Clark Prize at the National Academy. He showed in New York throughout his career; Ulrich also lived in Venice for many years. His paintings, popular for their exquisite brushwork and color, are strongly indebted to his Munich study. Ulrich died May 15, 1908, on a trip to Berlin.

Frank Waller was born in 1842 in New York City and received his first drawing lessons at the New York Free Academy, but he trained to be an architect. Waller went to Europe in 1870, meeting with John G. Chapman in Rome, and traveled abroad again in 1872, this time to Egypt where he made many studies which he was to use in later paintings. Waller attended the Art Students League, New York, in 1874, and subsequently became its treasurer and president, 1877–78. His *Report on Art Schools* was published in 1879. He did not make painting his full profession until 1903. He died in 1923 in New York City.

Charles Caleb Ward was born in St. John, New Brunswick, in 1830. The son of a successful merchant, he was sent to London as a young man to learn the family business. Ward studied with the watercolorist William Henry Hunt and painted several landscapes, which were exhibited at the National Academy of Design in 1850. Although he kept an address in New York during 1868–72, he probably spent most of his life in and around St. John, where the outdoors served as a model for his landscape and genre pictures. Ward was never well known or popular in his time. Perhaps due to adequate personal finances, he rarely sold a painting and his exhibitions at the National Academy of Design were few and far between. During Ward's later years, he suffered illness and increasing eye trouble, which seems to have affected his work. He died on February 24, 1896, in Rothesay, Kings County, Brooklyn.

John Ferguson Weir was born August 28, 1841, in West Point, New York. He received his early training from his father, Robert W. Weir, painter and art instructor at the West Point Military Academy. In 1861 Weir established his own studio in New York City. Celebrated for his dramatic use of industrial imagery, Weir urged his students to depict subjects relevant to American life. In 1866 Weir became an Academician at the National Academy of Design. From 1869 to 1913 he was Director of the Fine Arts School at Yale University, and in 1900 he received a medal at the Paris Exposition. Weir is also remembered for his essay "John Trumbull and His Work," 1902. Weir died on April 8, 1926, in Providence, Rhode Island.

Julian Alden Weir was born August 30, 1852, in West Point, New York, where he received art lessons from his father, Robert W. Weir, an instructor of art at the Military Academy. He also studied at the National Academy of Design, New York, 1867, and under Jean Léon Gérôme in Paris, 1874. Before establishing himself in New York as a painter, teacher, and tastemaker, Weir studied and traveled in Europe. In 1880, Weir first exhibited at the Paris Salon, receiving an honorable mention. An influential participant in the New York art world, Weir taught at the Art Students League from 1885–87, 1890–98, and was a founding member of the Society of American Artists, 1877, of Ten American Painters, 1898, and of the New Society, 1919. Among his most significant honors were his election to the National Academy of Design in 1885, and to the American Academy of Arts and Letters in 1919, and such awards as the Bronze Medal at the Paris Exposition, 1900; the Lippincott Prize at the Pennsylvania Academy of the Fine Arts, 1910; the Clark Prize and the Corcoran Gold Medal, 1914. The Metropolitan Museum of Art, New York, held a Weir retrospective following his death in New York on December 8, 1924.

James Abbott McNeill Whistler, though born in Lowell, Massachusetts, on July 11, 1834, chose to live and work for most of his life in London. Trained in Paris, he attended the Ecole Imperiale de Dessin in 1855 and the Académie Gleyre in 1856. In 1863 he exhibited at the Salon des Refusés and in 1865 he painted with Courbet, Monet, and Daubigny at Trouville. His first one-man show in London, 1874, established him as the notorious personality who, in 1878, sued Ruskin for libel. Winning the Ruskin trial, Whistler was encouraged to teach and preach his radical ideas about art. In the famous "Ten O'Clock Lecture" Whistler argued that art is foremost an arrangement of line, form, and color. In 1890 a collection of Whistler's writings were published under the title *The Gentle Art of Making Enemies*. In later years, he made several painting trips to Holland and the Mediterranean, winning such awards as the Gold Medal, Antwerp Exhibition, 1895, and the Grand Prix, Paris International, 1900. Whistler died in London on July 17, 1903.

Thomas Waterman Wood was born on November 12, 1823, in Montpelier, Vermont. He studied in Boston under Chester Harding in 1846, and in 1852 went to New York as a portraitist. With the assistance of Mr. Derbyshire, the Queen's Painter from Quebec, Wood received several important portrait commissions and thereby established his reputation. He worked in Quebec and Washington, D. C., and spent two years in Baltimore, where he began to paint genre pictures. In 1859 he went to Europe for two years and during the Civil War he traveled south, where he produced many of his noted war-life pictures. Wood settled permanently in New York in 1867, becoming President of the American Water Color Society, 1878; President of the National Academy of Design, 1891; and co-organizer of the New York Etching Club. He died in New York on April 14, 1903.

Richard Caton Woodville was born on April 30, 1825, to a prominent Baltimore family. He attended St. Mary's College there and possibly received instruction from the painter Alfred Jacob Miller. In 1842 Woodville's name appears in the University of Maryland Medical School registry, but there is no evidence of his further pursuit in this field. He went to Germany in 1845, attended the Düsseldorf Academy for a year, and then received private instruction from Carl Ferdinand Sohn for the remainder of his six-year stay. In 1851 Woodville moved to Paris; he spent the rest of his life there and in London. Though he revisited the United States only on two brief occasions, his work was frequently exhibited in its galleries and popularized by engravings which were distributed by the American Art-Union. Woodville died accidentally, from an overdose of medically prescribed morphine, in London on August 13, 1855.

Selected Bibliography

The Art Gallery, University of California, Santa Barbara. *William Merritt Chase (1849–1916)*. Text by Ala Story. Santa Barbara: University of California, 1964.

BAIGELL, MATTHEW. *A History of American Painting*. New York: Praeger Publishers, 1971.

BAUR, JOHN I. H. *American Painting in the Nineteenth Century: Main Trends and Movements*. New York: Praeger Publishers, 1953.

————. *Eastman Johnson, 1824–1906: An American Genre Painter*. Brooklyn: Institute of Arts and Science, 1940.

————. "Trends in American Painting, 1815–1865." In *M. and M. Karolik Collection of American Paintings, 1815 to 1865*. Cambridge, Massachusetts: Harvard University Press, 1949.

BENJAMIN, S. G. W. *Art in America: A Critical and Historical Sketch*. New York: Harper & Brothers, Publishers, 1880.

BLOCH, E. MAURICE. "The American Art-Union's Downfall." *The New-York Historical Society Quarterly*, XXXVII (1953), 331–59.

————. *George Caleb Bingham. Vol. I: The Evolution of an Artist. Vol. II: A Catalogue Raisonné*. Vol. VII of the *California Studies in the History of Art*. Berkeley and Los Angeles: University of California Press, 1967.

BOLTON-SMITH, ROBIN, and WILLIAM H. TRUETTNER. *Lilly Martin Spencer: The Joys of Sentiment*. Washington, D.C.: National Collection of Fine Arts, Smithsonian Institution, 1973.

BREESKIN, ADELYN D. *Mary Cassatt: A Catalogue Raisonné of the Oils, Pastels, Watercolors, and Drawings*. Washington, D.C., 1970.

BROWN, MILTON W. *American Painting from the Armory Show to the Depression*. Princeton, New Jersey: Princeton University Press, 1955.

City Art Museum of Saint Louis. *William Glackens in Retrospect*. Text by Leslie Katz. Saint Louis, Missouri: City Art Museum of Saint Louis, 1966.

CLARK, ELIOT. *History of the National Academy of Design: 1825–1953*. New York: Columbia University Press, 1954.

CLEMENT, C. E., and LAURENCE HUTTON. *Artists of the 19th Century and Their Works*. New York: Houghton Mifflin Company, 1879.

Corcoran Gallery of Art. *American Processional, 1492–1900*. Introduction by Hermann Warner Williams, Jr. Text by Elizabeth McCausland. Washington, D.C.: National Capital Sesquicentennial Commission, 1950.

CORN, WANDA M. *The Color of Mood: American Tonalism, 1880–1910*. San Francisco: M. H. de Young Memorial Museum and the California Palace of the Legion of Honor, 1972.

COWDREY, MARY BARTLETT. *American Academy of Fine Arts and American Art-Union, 1816–1852*. 2 vols. New York: The New-York Historical Society, 1953.

————. *National Academy of Design Exhibition Record, 1826–1860*. 2 vols. New York: The New-York Historical Society, 1943.

———— and HERMANN W. WILLIAMS, JR. *William Sidney Mount 1807–1868: An American Painter*. Published for The Metropolitan Museum of Art. New York: Columbia University Press, 1944.

CREER, DORIS J. "Thomas Birch: A Study of the Condition of Painting and the Artist's Position in Federal America." Unpublished master's thesis, University of Delaware, 1958.

CUMMINGS, THOMAS S. *Historic Annals of the National Academy of Design*. Philadelphia: George W. Childs, Publisher, 1865.

DOMIT, MOUSSA M. *American Impressionist Painting.* Washington, D.C.: National Gallery of Art, 1973.

DOWNES, WILLIAM HOWE. *The Life and Works of Winslow Homer.* Boston and New York: Houghton Mifflin Company, 1911.

FLEXNER, JAMES THOMAS. *That Wilder Image: The Painting of America's Native School from Thomas Cole to Winslow Homer.* Boston: Little, Brown, 1962.

FRANKENSTEIN, ALFRED. *Painter of Rural America: William Sidney Mount 1807–1858.* Introduction by Jane des Grange. Stony Brook, New York: Suffolk Museum & Carriage House, 1968.

Gallery of Modern Art including the Huntington Hartford Collection. *George Bellows: Paintings, Drawings, Lithographs.* Foreword by Margaret Potter. Introduction by Charles H. Morgan. New York: The Foundation for Modern Art, 1966.

GARDNER, ALBERT TEN EYCK. *Winslow Homer, American Artist: His World and His Work.* New York: Bramhall House, 1961.

GOODRICH, LLOYD. *The Graphic Art of Winslow Homer.* New York: The Museum of Graphic Art, 1968.

———. *Thomas Eakins: His Life and Work.* New York: Whitney Museum of American Art, 1933.

———. *Winslow Homer.* New York: The Macmillan Company, 1944.

GROCE, GEORGE C., and DAVID H. WALLACE. *The New-York Historical Society's Dictionary of Artists in America, 1564–1860.* New Haven, Connecticut: Yale University Press, 1957.

GRUBAR, FRANCIS. *Richard Caton Woodville: An Early American Genre Painter.* Washington, D.C.: The Corcoran Gallery of Art, 1967.

HARRIS, NEIL. *The Artist in American Society: The Formative Years, 1790–1860.* New York: George Braziller, Inc., 1966.

Harvard University William Hayes Fogg Art Museum. *New England Genre: Art in New England.* Introduction by Museum Class. Cambridge, Massachusetts: Harvard University Press, 1939.

HILLS, PATRICIA. *The American Frontier: Images and Myths.* New York: Whitney Museum of American Art, 1973.

———. *Eastman Johnson.* New York: Clarkson N. Potter, Inc., 1972.

———. "The Genre Painting of Eastman Johnson: The Sources and Development of His Style and Themes." Ph.D. dissertation, New York University, 1973.

HOOPES, DONELSON F. *The American Impressionists.* New York: Watson-Guptill Publications, 1972.

LANES, JERROLD. "Boston Painting 1880–1930." *Artforum* X (January, 1972), 49–51.

LARKIN, OLIVER W. *Art and Life in America.* New York: Rinehart & Company, Inc., 1949.

LERMAN, LEO. *The Museum: One Hundred Years and The Metropolitan Museum of Art.* New York: The Viking Press, 1969.

LYNES, RUSSELL. *The Art-Makers of Nineteenth Century America.* New York: Atheneum, 1970.

McCLINTON, KATHARINE MORRISON. *The Chromolithographs of Louis Prang.* New York: Clarkson N. Potter, Inc., 1973.

MANN, MAYBELLE. *Frances William Edmonds: Mammon and Art.* Ph.D. dissertation, New York University, 1972.

MARLOR, CLARK S. *A History of The Brooklyn Art Association with an Index of Exhibitions.* New York: James F. Carr, 1970.

The Metropolitan Museum of Art. *Life in America.* New York: The Metropolitan Museum of Art, 1939.

———. *19th-Century America: Paintings and Sculpture: An Exhibition in Celebration of the Hundredth Anniversary of The Metropolitan Museum of Art.* Introduction by John K. Howat and John Wilmerding. Texts by John K. Howat, Natalie Spassky, and others. New York: The Metropolitan Museum of Art, 1970.

MILLER, DOROTHY. *The Life and Work of David G. Blythe.* Pittsburgh: University of Pittsburgh Press, 1950.

MILLER, LILLIAN B. *Patrons and Patriotism: The Encouragement of the Fine Arts in the United States 1790–1860.* Chicago: The University of Chicago Press, 1966.

MOTT, FRANK LUTHER, *A History of American Magazines.* 5 vols. Cambridge, Massachusetts: The Belknap Press of the Harvard University Press, 1957.

MOUNT, WILLIAM SIDNEY. Unpublished journal. Collection of the Suffolk Museum & Carriage House, Stony Brook, New York. (Formerly in the Whitney Museum of American Art, New York and referred to as the "Whitney Journal.")

MUMFORD, LEWIS. *The Brown Decades: A Study of the Arts of America, 1865–1895.* 2d rev. ed. New York: Dover Publications, Inc., 1955. (First published in 1931.)

Museum of Art, Munson-Williams-Proctor Institute. *George Luks, 1866–1933.* Texts by Ira Glackens and Joseph S. Trovato. Utica, New York: Munson-Williams-Proctor Institute, 1973.

NAEVE, MILO M. "John Lewis Krimmel: His Life, His Art, and His Critics." Unpublished master's thesis, University of Delaware, 1955.

National Gallery of Art. *John Sloan, 1871–1951.* "His Life and Paintings," by David W. Scott. "His Graphics," by E. John Bullard. Washington, D.C.: National Gallery of Art, 1971.

NAYLOR, MARIA, ed. *The National Academy of Design Exhibition Record: 1861–1900.* 2 vols. New York: Kennedy Galleries, Inc., 1973.

NEUHAUS, EUGEN. *The History and Ideals of American Art.* Stanford, California: Stanford University Press, 1931.

New Jersey State Museum. *Everett Shinn, 1873–1953.* In-

troductions by Charles T. Henry, Ira Glackens, and Bennard B. Perlman. Annotated Chronology by Edith DeShazo. Trenton: New Jersey State Museum, 1973.

NOCHLIN, LINDA. *Realism*. Baltimore: Penguin Books, Inc., 1971.

NOVAK, BARBARA. *American Painting of the Nineteenth Century: Realism, Idealism, and the American Experience*. New York: Praeger Publishers, 1969.

PARRINGTON, VERNON LOUIS. *The Beginning of Critical Realism in America, 1860–1920*. New York: Harcourt, Brace and Company, 1930.

PARRY, ELLWOOD. *The Image of the Indian and the Black Man in American Art, 1590–1900*. New York: George Braziller, Inc., 1974.

PESSEN, EDWARD. *Jacksonian America: Society, Personality, and Politics*. Homewood, Illinois: Dorsey Press, 1969.

PETERSON, HAROLD L. *Americans at Home: From the Colonists to the Late Victorians*. New York: Charles Scribner's Sons, 1971.

PROWN, JULES DAVID. "Washington Irving's Interest in Art and His Influence upon American Painting." Unpublished master's thesis, University of Delaware, 1956.

RICHARDSON, E. P. *Painting in America: From 1502 to the Present*. New York: Thomas Y. Crowell Company, 1956.

ROSE, BARBABA, ed. *Readings in American Art Since 1900: A Documentary Survey*. New York: Praeger Publishers, 1968.

ROSENBERG, JAKOB, SEYMOUR SLIVE, and E. H. TER KUILE. *Dutch Art and Architecture: 1600–1800*. Baltimore: Penguin Books, Inc., 1966.

ROWLAND, BENJAMIN, JR. "Popular Romanticism: Art and the Gift Books." *The Art Quarterly*, XX (Winter, 1957), 364–81.

RUTLEDGE, ANNA WELLS. *Cumulative Record of Exhibition Catalogues: The Pennsylvania Academy of the Fine Arts, 1807–1870; the Society of Artists, 1800–1814; the Artists' Fund Society, 1835–1845*. Philadelphia: American Philosophical Society, 1955.

SCHENDLER, SYLVAN. *Eakins*. Boston: Little, Brown, 1967.

SCOTT, DAVID W., and E. JOHN BULLARD. *John Sloan: 1871–1951*. Washington, D.C.: National Gallery of Art, 1971.

SHANNON, FRED A. *The Centennial Years: A Political and Economic History of America from the Late 1870s to the Early 1890s*. 2d ed. Edited by Robert Huhn Jones. Garden City, New York: Anchor Books, 1969.

SPENCER, BENJAMIN T. *The Quest for Nationality*. Syracuse, New York: Syracuse University Press, 1957.

STEIN, ROGER B. *John Ruskin and Aesthetic Thought in America, 1840–1900*. Cambridge, Massachusetts: Harvard University Press, 1967.

SWEET, FREDERICK A. *Sargent, Whistler, and Mary Cassatt*. Chicago: Art Institute of Chicago, 1954.

TAYLOR, GEORGE ROGERS. *The Transportation Revolution 1815–1860*. New York: Harper & Row, 1968. (First published as Vol. IV, *The Economic History of the United States*. New York: Holt, Rinehart & Winston, 1951.)

TRUETTNER, WILLIAM H., and ROBIN BOLTON-SMITH. *National Parks and the American Landscape*. Washington, D.C.: National Collection of Fine Arts, Smithsonian Institution, 1972.

SHELDON, GEORGE W. *American Painters With Eighty-three Examples of Their Work Engraved on Wood*. London: Cassell Petter & Galpin; New York: D. Appleton & Company, 1878.

TUCKERMAN, HENRY T. *Book of the Artists: American Artist Life, Comprising Biographical and Critical Sketches of American Artists, Preceded by an Historical Account of the Rise and Progress of Art in America*. New York: James F. Carr, 1967. (First published in 1867.)

VAIL, R. W. G. *Knickerbocker Birthday: A Sesqui-centennial History of The New-York Historical Society, 1804–1954*. New York: The New-York Historical Society, 1954.

VEBLEN, THORSTEIN. *The Theory of the Leisure Class: An Economic Study of Institutions*. New York: The New American Library, 1953. (First published in 1899.)

WESTERVELT, ROBERT F. "The Whig of Missouri." *The American Art Journal* II, No. 1 (Spring, 1970), 46–53.

Whitney Museum of American Art. *Art of the United States: 1670–1966*. Text by Lloyd Goodrich. New York: Whitney Museum of American Art, 1966.

WILLIAMS, HERMANN WARNER, JR. *The Civil War: The Artists' Record*. Boston and Washington, D.C.: Museum of Fine Arts, Boston, and The Corcoran Gallery of Art, 1961.

———. *Mirror to the American Past: A Survey of American Genre Painting: 1750–1900*. Greenwich, Connecticut: New York Graphic Society Ltd., 1972.

WILMERDING, JOHN. *Winslow Homer*. New York: Praeger Publishers, 1972.

Index

Page numbers in italic denote illustrations.

Art Dept.

WP83+H559p

Hills
The painters'
~~ica.

Art Dept.

WP83+H559p

JUN 3 1976	FEB 1 0 1982	
JUL 3 1976	AUG 21 1982	
JUL 8 1976	SEP 1 3 1984	
	MAR 1 8 1986	
NOV 1 1976	NOV 2 9 1986	
DEC 6 1976	DEC 2 1988	
JAN 3 0 1977	JAN 2 5 1989	
MAR 1 9 1977	FEB 2 5 1989	
APR 2 2 1977	MAR 2 5 1989	
MAY 1 9 1977	APR 2 9 1989	
JUN 1 5 1977	OCT 2 3 1989	
NOV 2 3 1977	OCT - 1 1999	
JAN 9 1978		
MAR 2 1 1979		
AUG 2 5 1979		
SEP 1 8 1979		
MAR 3 1980		
AUG 1 9 1980		
JUL 1 3 1981		
JAN 1 8 1982		
NNH 2/82		